MICK BOGERMAN'S
WARNING NOTE TO PARENTS:

Hey, parents! It's me, Mick Bogerman. I'm here to tell you this story is rated PG for skin-searing lasers and fighting. Beware, the robots in this story will not vacuum your room. They will annihilate your room instead—with you in it. The language is standard twelve-year-old name-calling, like dorkhead, booger-breath, and slug-pie ugly, although I do make a special effort to stay clear of mom insults and potty jokes. As far as stupid romance, I tried my best to keep it out of this story, even though my brother had other ideas.

So, if you're looking for a wimpy, child-type book, turn away now. But if your kid is not a wimp, likes a heart-pounding scare and chasing down evil killer robots, then this, dear parent, is the story for your kid.

ALSO BY
MICK BOGERMAN

Slug Pie Story #1:

How to Navigate Zombie Cave and

Defeat Pirate Pete

Slug Pie Story #2:

How to Rid Your Swimming Pool of

a Bloodthirsty Mermaid

How to Destroy
the
New Girl's
Killer
Robot Army

Slug Pie Story #3

How to Destroy the New Girl's Killer Robot Army

Mick Bogerman

SLUG PIE STORIES, LLC

Slug Pie Stories, LLC
8126 West Evergreen Drive
Frankfort, IL 60423

www.slugpiestories.com

Book design © 2013, BookDesignTemplates.com

Cover design © 2014, Kat Powell

Cover illustration © 2014, Kat Powell

Frankfort / Mick Bogerman – First Edition

ISBN 978-0-9903801-6-0

Printed in the United States of America

For Darren

Tell the New Girl to Go Away

I ONCE READ about a guy who had his friends pack him into a box and then ship him to his girlfriend's house across town. If I had the money, I'd Fed-Ex Savannah Diamond all the way back to Jacksonville, Florida.

New kids at school are usually quiet and shy until they settle in with a group of friends. Not this girl. She's loud and bossy, and she loves to mess with my life.

Last week she outran me in gym class. I have a reputation to keep, and getting beat by a girl, well, it sucks. Then afterward, she called me a gastropod. I had to look the word up in the dictionary. Why she couldn't just say "snail" like a normal person? No, she's gotta beat me *and* make me feel stupid.

Well, I got her back good. Yesterday, I volunteered to hold her feet while she did sit-ups, and when she wasn't looking, I put two big wads of chewed gum on the bottoms of her sneakers. Boy did she get in trouble for tracking that sticky mess across the gym floor. She even had to stay after and clean it up.

Now she's taken over my favorite hangout, Eclipse Comic Emporium. What girl likes comic books? They're all supposed to be playing princess or dollies, not reading *X-Men*. Me and my brother used to go to the comic book store to get away from girls, but now Finley wants to go all the time to try to catch a glimpse of *her*.

He's been gaga stupid ever since that day he first saw her at the beach. There we were, sitting around, seeing how long it takes for spit to soak into the sand. Longer than you'd think, by the way. Finally, I said, "Finley. Let's go crabbing."

But he said, "Who's that over there? She's pretty."

I looked at the girl he was pointing at, and my mouth fell open. "Her? That's Van Demon. She's the new girl likes to make everyone feel dumb."

And right when I'm trying to explain why he should stay clear of Demon Girl, he ups and follows after her like a puppy, making friends. My stomach tosses just thinking about it. Well, I sure wasn't gonna hang around. Caught three huge crabs all by myself, while the two of them collected seashells and built a sandcastle. Had to practically drag him by the hair when it was time to go home.

"Bye, Finley," she said.

"Bye, Savannah," he said.

Ugh.

Later, after I had a chance to tell him what she's like at school, I asked for his help to get rid of her. Did he side with me? Support his own brother?

Nope.

His eyes got all moony and his face got all pink and he said, "I don't want her to leave. She's nice to me. Maybe if you were nice to her, she'd be nice to you too."

I'm older than him, for Pete's sake. I know more about girls than he does. "That is not how the world works, little brother," I told him.

Last night was the last straw. After dinner we were all watching TV together. At least I thought we were watching TV. But then I looked over at my brother and he was doodling in his notebook: Finley + Savannah. Inside a *heart*. Yuck.

Now that she's made my little brother fall into a crush coma, she's got to go. And before he starts putting our last name next to her first name in his notebook. Since I haven't been able to snap him back to reality, I'll have to talk sense into Van Demon herself. What exactly I'll say, I haven't decided yet, but "Go back where you came from" is likely a big part of it.

So here I am standing outside Mr. Gee's comics shop on a Saturday morning 'cause he told me that's when *she's* been stopping by all month. Well, once I set this girl straight and she runs crying back where she belongs, I'll grab the new *Avengers Assemble* myself and give it a look-see. It'll be my bonus for getting rid of Van Demon and will make the walk over totally worth it.

There! I cross my arms and glare as she speeds around the street corner. She comes up on me so fast, all I see is a flash of tan legs, bony elbows, and blonde hair. Her shiny, new boy's bike hops over the curb and skids to a stop an inch away from my feet. She catches me eyeballing her ride.

"Whatcha waiting for? Your mommy coming to pick you up 'cause your bike's busted?"

How Demon Girl even knows about my bike is hard to say. I busted it trying to catch a bloodthirsty mermaid this summer, had to leave it behind. Didn't get a chance to go back for it, but when I did a few weeks later, it had vanished. I put a new one on

Uncle George's list of stuff to get, but it's gonna be a while. Bikes aren't cheap.

"Yeah. Bet you're the one that stole it," I tell her. Could be true. She moved to town after me and Finley rescued the mermaid victims.

She flashes her eyes at me. "What would I want with your stupid, busted bike?" She wheels her own bike over to the side of the building and props it against the brick wall. Her bike's all polished new. It's got pinstriped flames on the top and down tubes. The seat's buffed and glossy. Even the chain looks newly oiled.

"I don't know. Use it for parts to build a killer robot army and rule the world."

"You're such an ignoramus, Mickey."

I wince when she says my full name. I go by Mick, and she very well knows it. And what the heck's an ignoramus?

"I wouldn't need your bike to do that." She slides her backpack off, letting it plop to the ground, and then she unzips the top like she's got something sinister hidden inside. Her hand reaches in and pulls out—a hairbrush. "Why are you talking to me, anyway?" She brushes the sweaty tangles out of her hair, shining it up like pirate treasure. "I know you hate my guts."

I don't argue. "I came to tell you to stay away from my brother. If you even talk to him again, you'll be sorry."

"Who? Finley?" She tucks her hairbrush into her backpack, grabs a rubber hair thing from a side pocket, and tugs her hair into a tight ponytail. "What's wrong with him?"

"What? Nothing's wrong with him."

"Then how come he can't talk anymore?"

"He can talk. I never said—"

"Does Finley know you're making up stories about him? Some brother you are."

My temple throbs like when Beginner Band is playing, except now it feels like Neill Gillis is marching with his tuba on my brain. "Cut it out!"

"Cut what out?"

"You're twisting my words."

"*Au contraire*, Mickey. Your words are twisted even before they shoot out of your mouth. You're the one can't talk right, not your brother. See ya'."

Her ponytail flicks my face as she pops open the door to Mr. Gee's store. Bells tinkle and the door slaps shut behind her.

"Ugh!" I ball my fists and stomp the sidewalk.

Now I can't even look through the new comics. *She's* in there.

An empty can rests on the curb and I kick it, hard, into the street. A car coming down Benton squashes it flat. I imagine it's Van Demon's face.

Get a Guard Dog

I DON'T HAVE MONEY for bus fare, and with no bike it takes me another hour to walk back to our apartment building. By the time I get home, I'm more thirsty than angry. Maybe there's Coke in the fridge.

As I trudge across the south parking lot, a dog howls loud and long like he's just swallowed a bowlful of grief. Sounds like the noise is coming from the patch of weeds we call a courtyard. When I get around the side of our building, I see him: the world's most miserable dog. And I can't blame him.

The Garnet twins have got him tied to the fire hydrant. They're dunking scrub brushes into buckets of soapy water and lathering the poor guy until his fur's a slick, matted mess.

"Hey," I call out. "Where'd you get the dog?" I get closer, and the dog looks at me like I'm gonna hurl more misery at him. I scratch his head, and his tail wags weakly before he tucks it back between his legs.

"We found him at the dump." Bridgett's clothes

are sudsy-soaked like she's been bathing herself as much as the dog.

Trish takes a brush and scours the dog's chin. He howls again.

I cover my ears. "Mr. Fouler won't let you keep him here. No pets allowed." I figure our super must be gone, 'cause the dog's noise would've had him storming outside all steaming and red-faced.

"Once he's clean and smelling good, Mr. Fouler will change his mind. We could use a good guard dog." Trish squirts more dish soap into the bucket and sloshes it around with the brush. "We'll keep Bagel Boy in the shed. It can be his doghouse."

"We can fix the shed up nice for him. With blankets and everything. If you help us, he can be your dog too." Bridgett grins like it's all settled.

"Bagel Boy?" Figures the twins would come up with the worst dog name in the history of the universe.

"He loves bagels. We gave him a whole package, and he ate every one."

"Ten of them."

"You love your name, don't you Bagel Boy?" Trish says in baby talk.

The dog perks his ears.

"See?"

"When you say 'bagel,' he thinks you're gonna feed him again. Looks like he's missed a few meals." I brush my fingers along the dog's side and feel ribs through his wet fur.

"Don't worry. We got lots of food for him. Mama went shopping yesterday. We got bacon and apples and Cheetos."

Poor dog is gonna puke his guts out in no time. "Well, don't get your heart set on keeping him." Mr. Fouler isn't known for his kind heart. Threatening eviction? Yes. Kindness? No.

"Hey, Mick, where you going? Ain't you gonna help?"

Ah, man. I shake my head as I cross the courtyard. What've those girls duped me into now? "Yeah. I'll be back with some blankets. And I'll clean out a spot in the shed."

Another howl pierces the air. I look over my shoulder. Bridgett's holding the bucket over the dog. The last of the suds dribble onto his soaked head. Without warning, he twists and shakes, spraying the twins with a shower of scum.

"Good one, Boy," I mutter. The door closes behind me, muffling the girl's squeals.

In our apartment, Mom left a note that she and

Finley went to the YMCA for his swim lesson. My brother's been going every week on Uncle George's dime, and he's getting good. I went with them last Saturday to watch. His teacher says a couple more levels and he'll be ready for the swim team. Who would've thought after I saved him from drowning so many times that he'd be the one to end up on the swim team? Crazy.

The bus won't get them back until late this afternoon, so I'm on my own for lunch. No Coke, but I guzzle a half bottle of apple juice and then chase that with a couple glasses of cold water. I slap together a peanut butter sandwich and scarf it down with one hand while I pull a couple blankets from the closet with the other hand.

By the time I get back outside, the twins have let the dog off the rope, and he isn't cooperating. He sprints back and forth like a rabbit, until he's got equal distance from them both, and then screeches to a stop to roll in the dry weeds. In a moment he's back up and running, his tongue hanging, bits of leaves clinging to his damp fur.

I toss the blankets on the ground and make myself comfortable. I expect to watch this game for a while. But as soon as I sit, the dog hurtles over and plunks his wet self on the clean, dry blankets, his head on his outstretched legs. I pat his scraggly fur and that's when I see them.

Lice.

I've seen them before, on Finley. Three years ago his whole second grade class got sent home, and Mom quarantined him in our bedroom for days. I had to sleep on the couch while he scratched all night.

There's no mistaking, this dog's got lice.

Bridgett and Trish wander over pink-faced and out of breath. Trish must notice my nose crinkling or my mouth frowning 'cause she says, "What's wrong?"

"Someone's gotta go to the vet and get some lice-killing stuff."

"Lice?"

"Yeah, your dog has it bad. Takes days to get rid of, too."

"That's silly. Only people get lice." Bridgett plops on the ground next to us.

"No, people get people lice, and dogs get dog lice."

"Can people get dog lice?" Trish asks.

"Naw. When my brother had lice, I researched it on the computer at the library. They look the same unless you put 'em under a magnifier. But dog lice only like to suck on dog blood, and people lice only like to suck on people blood. It's not like mosquitoes. Mosquitoes don't care what kind of blood they get."

"Ew, gross. I don't wanna talk about blood." Bridgett grabs her elbows and squeezes herself. "You should go to the vet for us. You can borrow my skateboard."

Sure wish I had my bike, but a skateboard's better than nothing. "OK, go get it. And bring back some money with you. Lice killer won't be free."

Bridgett tears off, and the dog raises his head to watch her go. She's fast. In no time she runs back carrying the skateboard and what looks like her mom's purse. She pulls out the wallet. "Mom's on the phone, so she was easy to mess with. She says we can have the ten-dollar bill." Bridgett hands me the money.

"Hope it's enough." I clutch the skateboard and pocket the cash. The dog rises to follow me. "No. Stay, Boy. If the vet sees you, he'll charge a thousand bucks to fix you."

"Bagel Boy," Trish says.

I don't say a word. I will never call anyone or anything *Bagel Boy.*

Getting to the vet is no trouble. I was there just last month when my friend PJ's kitten got her shots.

No, the trouble isn't getting to the vet. The trouble is the idea that won't let go of me the whole time I'm getting there: without a magnifying glass, dog lice and people lice look the same. A spark of vengeance lights in the back of my brain, and before you can say, "dog lice in a demon's hairbrush," I've got a full-blown plan to get Savannah Diamond out of my school and out of my life.

Start the War

I GO OVER MY PLAN for getting rid of Van Demon the whole way back from the vet. It's a tricky set up, requiring perfect timing and ninja stealth, but if I can defeat pirate zombies, I can certainly defeat a snarky girl.

I'm so distracted thinking about it, I nearly crash-land the skateboard on top of the twins. And their mom.

"Sorry!" I crane my neck up.

Mrs. Garnet is the tallest woman I know. And skinny like a broom handle. "This dog is a mess," she says.

Bridgett clasps her hands together like she's praying. "Mama, please can we keep him?"

"He won't be any trouble." Trish hiccups and makes her lower lip quiver at the same time.

"We'll keep him in the shed," Bridgett says.

"Please, Mama. They'll murder him at the pound. We can save his life." Trish touches her mom's arm.

The girls are laying it on thick. We've got three

no-kill shelters around town. The dog's not going on death row.

Mrs. Garnet looks at the dog. Then she looks at her girls. Then back at the dog. Her mouth softens first.

The dog sits right in front of her and lifts his paw to shake.

Mrs. Garnet wilts.

"Oh, all right. I'll talk to Mr. Fouler. Hopefully I can change his mind about pets. In the meantime, run and get that comb I use on tangles. The one with the teeth wide apart. It'll be yours now," she says to the dog. "And some scissors. These mats will need to be cut out."

"Thank you, Mama. Thank you!" The twins run to our building and disappear inside.

Mrs. Garnet shakes her head and sighs. "You'll do the lice application after I trim his fur."

I say, "OK," even though she didn't exactly ask me.

She kneels by the dog and he licks her hand. "There's a sucker born every second, Mick. Happy birthday to me."

"Yes, ma'am." Not sure if I'm agreeing that she's a sucker, or maybe today really is her birthday.

❖ ❖ ❖

Once Mrs. Garnet finishes grooming the dog, she disappears inside to take a phone call and feed the girls their dinner, leaving me to apply the lice medicine. I crouch next to the dog and start picking through his fur, close to his skin. There they are, looking like specks of dirt. Behind his ears. In his leg pits. Underneath his tail. Not a nice place for an itch.

"Boy, you must be miserable."

I pluck off as many lice as I can find and drop them into a plastic bag I snagged from the kitchen. I use my mom's tweezers to scrape and pull off some of the nits, too. They might not last long sealed up in an airtight plastic bag. But for what I have planned, dead or alive won't matter. It won't matter that they're the dog kind, either.

People go nutzoid about lice. Especially *school* people. They FREAK OUT. School people won't take the time to research what kind of lice these are. They won't compare lice types with a magnifying glass. They'll never know they came from a dog. If they're on a person, they'll automatically think they're the people kind of lice.

Once I have enough ammunition, I take out the

tube of lice killer and unscrew the red cap. Time to help the poor dog. The vet said the stuff will kill the lice, and fleas and ticks too, for a whole month.

Mom and Finley get back just as I'm introducing the dog to his new bed of blankets in the shed. I tie his rope to Mr. Fouler's tool chest.

Finley peers into the shed. "A dog. A dog. A dog." He bounces on his toes like he's three instead of nine.

"Does Mr. Fouler know about him yet?" Mom gestures at the dog.

"Mrs. Garnet says she'll talk to Mr. Fouler."

The dog circles a couple times and then curls into a tight ball onto the blankets, resting his head on his back legs.

"Well, he looks sweet enough. Does he make a lot of noise?"

"Not since his bath. Hasn't made a sound."

"Maybe that will work in his favor."

We leave the dog, who's now unconscious. Probably exhausted after his rescue and extreme makeover.

"What'd the Garnets name him?" Finley asks.

"I'll tell you when we get inside." I know Finley's laughter will wake the poor dog up. Hopefully drywall and brick will muffle the sound.

❖ ❖ ❖

Monday at school I pretend to dig through my locker while I watch for Savannah. Her locker isn't far from mine. She doesn't even look my way, just grabs a book and her pencil case and bounds off to class. I wait a few minutes until everyone's cleared the hallway. Then I make my move.

Easy access when I know she uses 1-2-3 for the combination. She might use big words and be book smart, but the practical stuff—not so bright. She is a neat freak, though. Not like my locker where the door won't even shut 'cause my stuff's in the way.

Her backpack hangs on a hook, and I know right where she keeps that hairbrush of hers. Golden strands wind around the bristles. I shake out half the contents of the plastic bag onto the brush and push a few of the critters deep into the base. I tuck her brush back where it belongs, zip the pocket closed, latch her locker shut, and give the dial on her lock a spin.

I skid into first period with Mrs. Shumaker. Her nostrils pinch as she pulls out her pad of pink slips. When she's done writing, she rips the paper off the pad with a flourish and waves it at me.

"Make sure this gets to Principal Nuñez before lunch."

I stuff the slip into my back pocket. "Yes, ma'am." No sense apologizing when she gets so much enjoyment out of writing me up. I should say, "You're welcome."

Savannah sits diagonal in front of me, so I have to walk past her and behind her to take my seat next to Booger-Face MacDougal. I avoid catching her glance. I'm sure she's smirking at me. She always does.

Smirk away, Demon Girl. Today's your last day at this school. Phase one is already complete. Get ready for phase two.

I fidget through class, barely paying attention to Mrs. Shumaker droning on about wagon trains and buffalo. I get it. Life on the prairie was tough. Churning your own butter? Yay for the Industrial Revolution. The minutes tick. The seconds tock. The clock pasted on the wall at the front of the classroom slows down whenever I watch.

Almost. Almost.

My timing has to be perfect. I remove the plastic bag and dump the lice leftovers into my hand, keeping everything hidden under my desk. Then from my pocket I add the best part: tiny dead beetles and some dead baby spiders for effect. Found 'em in the corner of the laundry room in the basement this morning. The lice are too small; I needed bugs big enough to see from a couple feet away. The bugs feel gritty, like dirt in my palm.

At 9:44:58 a.m., I jump to my feet and reach across my desk. Mrs. Shumaker says, "Mick, the bell hasn't–" and then the class bell rings right at 9:45:00 a.m. Other students push back their chairs and start to get up, but not Savannah. She's carefully putting her pencil back in her pencil case, like she always does. I brush off my hands and watch the little critters fall onto the back of Savannah's head. Some of them roll right off, but enough brown specks stick to her light-colored hair that you can see them if you look. Phase two complete.

Now for phase three. I scoot behind Booger-Face MacDougal and nudge with my elbow.

"What?" He swings around.

"Savannah's got something crawling in her hair," I whisper at him.

Perfect timing.

Savannah stands to leave, and just as Booger-Face looks, one of the bugs drops off her head and lands on the desk.

"Cooties! Bugs! Savannah's got 'em crawling on her." Booger-Face points at a tiny dark bug on the tan desktop. "That one just flew off her head."

Turning and whirling, Savannah looks this way and that.

Marissa Manning screeches. "Her hair is full of them. EEEWW! Get away. Get away!" She pushes past the rest of us and disappears out the door.

Savannah runs her hands through her hair. "Where? Where?" Another bug drops onto the desk behind her.

Brendan Pipitone sees and shouts, "Mrs. Shumaker, come quick. Savannah's infected!"

And then like dominoes . . .

"Stay away!" a girl yells.

"Don't let her touch you."

"Cooties!"

Kids pile up at the door, pushing to get out.

Mrs. Shumaker strides over to Savannah, nostrils flaring this time. "What's going on here?"

Brendan pipes up. "Savannah's infected with bugs."

"No I'm not!" She narrows her eyes and sticks her chin out.

"Let me look." Mrs. Shumaker pushes her glasses from the tip of her nose onto the bridge. She inspects Savannah's head. "There's definitely something there.

Could be a case of lice. Do you have any hats, hair-brushes, or combs with you?"

"In my backpack. In my locker." Savannah's voice comes out tiny, like she suddenly shrunk three feet.

"Come with me." Mrs. Shumaker grabs Savannah's arm and escorts her to the front of the room.

The kids clear out of the way. They whisper between their fingers and stare. Some point, some snicker.

Savannah's cheeks flush pink. Her eyes widen, her gaze darts from face to face, and her fingers clutch her pencil case as Mrs. Shumaker ushers her out the door.

Out of my life, I remind myself. And out of Finley's life, too.

So how come I feel like I ate spoiled potato salad?

STEP 4

Endure the Aftermath

MY PLAN WENT MUCH better in my head than in real life. In my head, Van Demon gets kicked out of school for a few days while her parents fumigate and sterilize her. She's so humiliated by the experience that her parents have to homeschool her, or send her to the Catholic school in the next town over, or rich boarding school like where PJ goes. It ends up being such a burden on her family that they sell their house and move away. Problem solved.

In real life, the whole middle school gets checked for lice, one head at a time. The line outside the nurse's office stretches down the hall and into the gym. Teachers have to help check heads. Even Mrs. Durtliff, our cafeteria lady, gets in on the bug search.

The whole day ends up being a bummer. Since the teachers are busy, they can't teach. The gym's occupied. We aren't allowed to hang outside with no one to supervise. So we sit at our homeroom desks and read, scribble, and sleep.

When I get home, Mom's got an early dinner set out, which is strange, 'cause she's usually not home from her job at the grocery store until later.

"Guess what happened at school today, Mick?" Finley asks before shoveling a spoonful of sausage and rice into his mouth.

I think I know, but I let him go ahead and tell me while I stir my meal, releasing a cloud of steam. Smells awesome.

"We got checked for lice again. Just like last time. Only this time I don't got any."

"Have any. You don't *have* any." Mom frowns at me.

"Yeah. I got the all clear." Finley sprays bits of rice when he talks.

Mom frowns at me again, like it's my fault the kid's got no table manners and no grammar.

"False alarm at your school, but Mick's school sent twenty kids home. The nurse left us a message."

I scrape the last bit of rice out of my bowl. Twenty kids. I sure didn't expect that. Maybe they all did have the real bugs. Good thing I framed Savannah; otherwise, those other kids wouldn't have been found out. We could've had–

"An epidemic, if it's not caught early." Mom clears her dishes.

I don't remember seeing her eat, but the food's gone and she's cleaning up.

"You're awful quiet," she says when I join her at the sink.

That's her cue for me to tell her what's on my mind. Since a lecture and getting grounded forever are not on my wish list, I say, "Did Mr. Fouler decide anything about the dog?"

Mom shakes her head. "It doesn't look good. He was going to call Animal Control until Patty said she'd pay extra rent for him to stay in the shed." She squeezes soap into the sink and runs the hot water.

"Isn't that good news?"

"We'll see at the end of the month if she comes up with the extra money."

We start our nightly dishwashing assembly line. Mom washes, I rinse and dry, Finley puts away.

"I saw Savannah today." Finley slides the dried spoons into the utensil drawer. "She's always nice to me." His cheeks pink up and he grins like a goofball.

The glass I'm rinsing slips, but I catch it before it crashes against the edge of the sink. "How'd you manage that?" Finley only sees Savannah on the weekends around town or at the beach—not any places he'd have been at today.

"Mr. Diamond subbed math class for Miss Penny today. Savannah and her mom picked him up when school was done."

"The Diamonds gave your brother a ride." Mom hands me a soapy-slick plate.

This time the dish slips right between my fingers and hits the floor, splintering into three big pieces and a handful of tiny shards.

"Mick!" Mom stoops and gingerly picks up the pieces. "Don't move. Need to sweep this up." She leaves for a second and comes back with a dustpan and broom. "Hold, please."

I squat and position the dustpan for her. "Sorry, Mom."

"Accidents happen." She sweeps the shards. "You are awfully preoccupied today. Anything you want to talk about?"

"Why would you let Finley get a ride from the Diamonds? Especially with Savannah." The demon. "She's got lice," I add.

"It's my fault," Finley says. "I was getting on my bus, and I saw Savannah in the parking lot. She was hugging her dad and crying fierce. Like somebody died. I couldn't help it. I had to make sure she was OK. The bus left without me."

He takes the pan of shards from me, and I don't put up a fight. If he didn't take that pan, I'd probably still be there holding it with my mouth hanging open.

"Gary—Mr. Diamond—called me at work, and they dropped Finley off at the grocery store on their way home," Mom says.

"But . . . the lice?"

"Gary said it was curious that everything, nits and eggs, brushed right out of Savannah's hair and then they were gone. I told him when Finley had lice, those buggers clung to hundreds of individual strands all over his head. They wouldn't just brush out. They'd found a home and weren't going to leave willingly."

Actually, it isn't curious at all. Dog lice don't stick to people. They only stick to dogs. Savannah might be a demon, but she's still a human demon. Plus, the lice had to be mostly dead from spending the weekend inside a plastic bag. I bite down hard so my tongue doesn't give me away.

"The Diamonds bought the lice products anyway, but I checked her head myself. She looked clear from lice to me."

So much for my plan to get Savannah away from me and Finley. Now her family's best buds with my family. Riding around together. Talking with first names. How could this happen?

"Ugh."

Mom and Finley look at me like there's something wrong with me.

"I'll be in my room." I trudge off. I can feel their gazes boring holes into my back.

❖ ❖ ❖

After Finley settles into the bunk below me, Mom says good-night and heads off to her second job. Our fan hums along with the crickets outside. A couple moths cling to the screen. The night's cooler than it's been in a while, so our room actually feels nice. Good sleeping weather. If I can finally get Demon Girl outta my head so I can get some sleep.

"Mick?" Finley whispers. "You awake?"

"Yeah."

"What's wrong?"

"Nothing."

Cricket song swells outside and rings in my ears. I stare at the dark ceiling, but all I see are Van Demon's red-rimmed eyes.

"You're lying."

"Go to sleep."

"You did something bad."

"No."

The bed below creaks and the sheets rustle. "Then how come you're acting same as when you snagged the candy from The Lolly Shop?"

"I went back the next day and paid."

"Yeah, but you moped the whole night. Like now."

Darn those crickets are loud. I can hardly think straight. Where are the bullfrogs and snakes when you need them?

"I did what I had to do, and it didn't work out exactly, but I'm not sorry. I'm not."

"What'd ya' do?"

"Quit pestering me."

"I think you're sorry."

The crickets scream now. I remember Van Demon's eyes filling with tears and I squeeze my own eyes shut. "Enough already." I face the wall and stuff the pillow around my head.

"It must be bad. Will the police come for you?"

"Agh! I put dog lice in Savannah's hair and her brush so she'd get kicked outta school. Now leave. Me. Alone."

Finley gasps. Then he tumbles out of bed, dragging his pillow, and slams our door behind him.

The cricket noise dies down once Finley and his questions leave. The quiet feels even worse. I roll around in bed. The sheets lump into a ball at my feet. The moment I drift off, I swear bugs crawl across my face. I look at the clock glowing 2:00 a.m. on the dresser below. Staring at the ceiling, I count imaginary sheep as they jump over my bed, but they keep stopping to scratch themselves. I bury my head under my pillow. By 4:00 a.m., I give up, turn on the light, and dig through my comics. Hopefully Mom will see the dark circles under my eyes and let me skip school tomorrow. I mean today. She'll let me skip school today.

❖ ❖ ❖

"Have fun ditching school?" Finley grabs an apple from the fridge.

He must still be mad, 'cause snark is not his thing. It's better than silence, though.

"If it makes you feel better, no, I did not have fun. I got all my homework done."

He smirks. The expression doesn't look good on him.

"When are you going to stop being mad at me?"

"I'm not mad at you." He chews the apple with his mouth open. Crunching fills the room.

"Yes you are."

"Nope." *Crunch, crunch.*

I decide pummeling him won't help, so I try something else. "You shouldn't let a girl come between us."

He stops crunching, and I see something in his eyes I've never seen before: coldness. Like he doesn't care about me anymore. Feels like getting your palm sliced open when you pull a knife the wrong way out of the sink.

Maybe if I push a couple of his buttons, I can get that look to go away. "Well, this'll all be over when the Diamonds move away."

"The Diamonds are NOT gonna move." He shakes his apple at me. "Beachwood is their home now. Savannah belongs here. Her mom's gonna run for city councilwoman, and Mr. Diamond's up for a full-time job at my school." Finley's gaze goes from ice to fire.

A little relief slips through me. Mad I can deal with.

But then he says, "You're a dumbnut if you think they're gonna leave town because of what you did. Mr. Diamond says he's not leaving out of principle."

"What's that supposed to mean?"

"He says no one should back down to a bully."

"Who's bullying Mr. Diamond?"

"You."

No. No. No. If Mr. Diamond thinks I'm a bully, it can only mean one thing. My heart pounds on triple-fast play. If Finley tells me what I think he's gonna tell me, my head's gonna pop.

He crunches on the last of his apple. "You think you can do whatever you want to get your own way, but you're wrong." He chews for ten thousand minutes. He swallows, and I swear I can see that mushed-up apple squeeze down his gullet. "What you did was wrong. You never think before you do something. You'll never change." He throws that awful, stinking apple core away. Then he says it. In slo-mo.

"I told Mr. Diamond what you did."

Win the First Battle

THE MINUTE I WALK through the school door, I expect Principal Nuñez to grab me by my collar and drag me into his office. He'll talk in that über calm voice of his when he suspends me. Or worse, expels me. But he glides right by me in the hallway. In fact, nobody pays me any attention at all. Except when I turn in my homework. I get a raised eyebrow in history from Mrs. Shumaker and a gasp from my math teacher.

Lunch is normal, too. Booger-Face MacDougal sits with me and yammers about NASCAR. I nod and chew. Other than that, I'm pretty much under the radar today.

Mr. Diamond mustn't have told anyone yet. I wonder why. Maybe he's gonna tell Mom first. He knows when she works at the grocery store. He'll catch her there. Or he's biding his time, getting forensic evidence, sending Savannah's hairbrush to a lab to get tested. Then he'll turn me in to the police. Or Savannah and him are at the police right now. They'll get a warrant and handcuff me before I get to last period.

If keeping me in suspense is his plan, it's working. My arm hairs stand up tall waiting for someone to say something. Wondering who'll be the first to point and shout, "It was him! He brought lice to school. He's the bully!"

I go home on the bus without getting arrested and arrive before my ex-brother Finley, which gives me a chance to claim our room. For the first time in my life, I lock our door to keep him out. Mom will make me open up when she gets home from the grocery store. But once she leaves for her night job, the traitor can sleep on the couch again.

Since I disowned him yesterday for ratting me out to Mr. Diamond, me and Finley haven't done more than grunt at each other. Mom'll eventually force us to make up, but I can't imagine things will ever be the same. I tried to protect him, and he betrayed me. There's no going back from that.

There's no one I can rip about it with, either. PJ always sides with Finley, so I won't call him. There's my friends Mr. Gee at the comic book store or Karl Wheetly, the fisherman, but they're adults. Adults won't understand. Booger-Face MacDougal won't be a good listener either. Most of what I say to him goes through his head instead of sticking between his ears. Finley's the person I used to talk to.

I pull out *New Mutants #48* from my stack of comics and read until Mom calls me out for dinner. Finley doesn't beg to come in or jiggle the door handle once. Infuriating.

We sit across from each other at the table, Mom in the middle, eating slices of taco pie. Well, I don't exactly eat. Mom's a great cook and everything, but I'm not hungry, so I only pick at mine. I glance over at Finley, and he's stabbing at his.

Mom might be tired and distracted all the time from working two jobs, but us not eating our food? This she notices, all right.

"You two have until the weekend to work out your differences. Uncle George is coming the end of the month, but only if you've made up. Otherwise, I'll call him and tell him you two are too busy fighting for him to visit. Understand?"

I nod and imagine Finley nods too. I don't know for sure 'cause I don't look at him.

"Clean up after yourselves. I'm going to take a bath. I had to scrub out the seafood display cases today." She puts her plate in the sink and leaves.

Silence smothers the kitchen.

I can't take it. I wrap my leftovers in foil and stick them in the fridge. Uncle George might bring a bike for me this month. Am I willing to give that up to stay mad at Finley? I glance at my brother again. He's still stabbing dinner.

I can always walk.

❖ ❖ ❖

In my dreams a mournful howl shoots up my spine and explodes inside my ribcage. My heart pounds me awake. Wait. No. Someone's pounding on my door.

Takes me a second to shake the sleep away. My clock says it's almost midnight. My door pounds again.

Finley. Trouble.

"I'm coming!" I slide down my ladder, leap to the door, and unlock it.

Finley flings it forward, almost smashing it into me.

"Watch out, jeez. What's wrong?"

"Bagel Boy."

The howl stops us both short.

"He'll wake up Mr. Fouler." Finley tugs on my sleeve, urging me forward.

"OK, OK. Get your shoes." I don't bother changing

into clothes. I squish my feet into my gym shoes.

Finley's heels hang over the back of his, but there's no time to fix it 'cause the dog howls again. Mr. Fouler's gonna make us get rid of him for sure.

We dash out the door, tumble through the hall and down the stairs, and crash out of the building. Mr. and Mrs. Garnet and the twins pour out of their side of the building. Trish's sparkly gym shoes flash pink lightning when she walks. Me and Finley get to the shed first.

By the glow of the moon, I see the strangest sight. And I'm an expert on strange.

The dog has something pinned under its two front paws. The thing is part toaster oven, part colander, part electric razor. There's bike chains, steak knives, potato peelers, and tongs. All these pieces and parts are attached to each other with bolts and screws, and electrical wiring is strung through the whole thing.

"Whatcha got there, Boy?" I move in closer.

The thing under the dog's feet moves.

It moves!

It keeps moving.

It tries to sit up.

The dog stomps it back down and howls.

"What the . . ." Mr. Garnet comes up behind me. "Is that a—?"

"Robot!" Trish hollers.

"Goodness gracious. Where did it come from?" Mrs. Garnet squeezes into our semicircle at the entrance to the shed.

"Hey, Mick," Finley whispers. "Isn't that the basket from your bike?"

Sure enough, wrapped around the robot's chest like a square suit of armor is the wire basket I used to carry stuff on the back of my bike.

Mr. Garnet turns to me and says, "Did you make this thing?"

"No." I move my foot near the robot to poke it with the toe of my shoe.

The robot swipes at me with steak-knife fingers, nearly nicking my ankle.

"Whoa." I stumble back, laughing. What's the little robot man think it's gonna do? Chop me up?

The dog clamps his mouth around the robot's wrist and starts growling and shaking his head like he's got a new chew toy.

"Go, Bagel Boy!" Bridgett shouts.

The dog rips the robot's hand off and flings it aside. Sparking wires dangle from its arm. The hand twitches and lies still.

The robot's mouth glows, and a girl's voice comes out of the robot's head: "Retreat. Retreat."

"Is that a cell phone in its mouth?" Mrs. Garnet leans over the robot.

"Don't get too close, dear," Mr. Garnet advises.

"What's going on here?" Mr. Fouler's voice rings in the night. His robe flaps behind him as he crosses the courtyard.

Instinctively, our little crowd turns our backs to the dog and the robot, shielding them from view.

Mr. Fouler's belly continues to jiggle even after he stops in front of us. "Well?"

"Our dog stopped a prowler." Mrs. Garnet steps in front of Mr. Fouler. "He woke us to let us know. See for yourself."

What happens next happens so fast it's hard to believe it happens at all: Mr. Garnet and the twins part so Mr. Fouler can see inside the shed. The dog leaves the robot to jump on Mr. Fouler, paws on the man's shoulders, tongue slapping the man's chin. The robot leaps up, and in a flash of metal parts it scurries past our legs and disappears into the dark.

"Don't let it get away!" Mr. Garnet runs after the robot but stops when it's obvious the robot is long gone.

"Someone get this dog off of me." Mr. Fouler and the dog look like they're dancing.

"Come on, Bagel Boy. Good dog." Bridgett fixes the dog's blankets, and he drops off Mr. Fouler and curls into them.

"Was it a kid?" Mr. Fouler stares after the robot's path while he wipes slobber off his face with his sleeve. "Was short like a kid. Wearing a Halloween costume or something."

Everyone looks at each other. No one says a word.

"Brought knives, too?" Mr. Fouler approaches what's left of the robot's hand and then kicks it with his slippered foot. "What's happening to this town?"

He turns on his heel, reaches down to pat the dog's head, and says, "Good Boy." As he strides back to the building, he calls over his shoulder, "The dog can stay. For free."

I catch Finley's gaze and we smile at each other. I can't help it. There's nothing better than seeing a grouch soften up for man's best friend.

❖ ❖ ❖

"I'm still mad at you." Finley plops on his bed.

I climb the ladder to the top bunk and stretch out on the covers. At least he can admit it now.

"Feeling's mutual, kiddo." I don't think we've called a truce, but for now, we're talking. Good thing, since it's not every day we've got a robot to talk about. "So, did you hear that voice coming outta its head?"

"Yeah. Sounded like a girl. Do you think it was a recording?"

"I don't think so. I saw a phone inside its head. An iPhone or something. Like what PJ's got."

Finley shifts and the wood creaks. "PJ's has got a camera in it."

He's right. A camera. Maybe whoever controlled the robot could hear us and see us.

"Do you think it's like Mr. Fouler said? It was here to rob him?"

"Maybe. He's the only one worth robbing around here." Even our mom's cookie jar money is down to a few bucks.

"Bagel Boy wasn't tied up. Do you think he caught the robot in the shed or dragged it to the shed from somewhere else?"

"Don't know." I hadn't even thought of *that*. Finley's detective wheels must be spinning.

Finley clicks his tongue behind his teeth. "If it wanted to steal something from the shed, Mr. Fouler's tools are probably valuable. 'Cept the tool cabinet's heavy and has a lock."

I don't tell him I've picked Mr. Fouler's lock a bunch of times. How else could I fix my bike, Finley's skates, and the kitchen sink for Mom? "Maybe it was headed to the apartment building for something more valuable than tools."

"Like what?"

"Money. Credit cards. Jewelry. That robot was too small to steal something big like a computer or a TV." What else could it take? What else could it want?

"Or maybe it was snooping before the real crooks came. Like, um, like . . ."

"Scouting? Surveillance? A stakeout?"

"Yeah." Finley yawns. "And then maybe the crooks won't come here 'cause now they know we've got a dog." I hear him roll onto his side.

"That's gotta be it." Of course! Criminals are getting smarter all the time. It'd make sense they'd use technology to scope out their targets before they robbed them.

Mystery solved.

Survive a Close Call

SAVANNAH DEMON should've come back to school today, but she's nowhere to be found. Cooper Schwartz came back. He's sitting at our table devouring a lunch that could feed all of Beachwood. Neill Gillis and Caleb Tyner are back, too.

"Anybody seen Savannah?" I ask the guys. Did my plan work after all?

"Lice Girl?" Booger-Face stuffs a handful of cheese puffs into his mouth. A fluorescent-orange ridge stretches across his bottom lip.

Cooper swallows a hunk of sandwich and joins in. "Yeah, Grace said that Maggie said she overheard Mrs. Shumaker say to Mrs. Krevitch that Savannah's brush was crawling with them. Grace said Maggie said that Mrs. Shumaker told Mrs. Krevitch that she put on her driving gloves before she dropped the brush into an airtight bag. Grace said Maggie said—"

"Got it," I interrupt, 'cause somebody has to before next week.

"She won't show her face around here for a while. Not since everyone knows she's the one infected me and the whole school." Cooper slugs his milk. "That's a worse rep than Booger-Face's got."

Booger-Face smiles, showing off the orange grout between his teeth. "I came up with the name Lice Girl. Good one, huh?"

"Real creative." Yep. Van Demon has a new name now. From Booger-Face, of all people.

And it's caught on.

All morning, kids by their lockers, kids in class, kids in the washroom were talking about Lice Girl. I wish I'd made Van Demon stick. I'd rather be known as a demon than a lice girl any day. Well, for me it'd be Lice Guy. Of course, once the Diamond family tells the school what I did, that's exactly what I'll be known as: Lice Guy. Bug Guy. Black-Hearted-Evil-Enemy-Bullying-Insect Guy.

"Dude, you're a downer today." Booger-Face takes his tray to the garbage. The rest of us clear out too.

What follows is one of the worst days ever. In gym class, I miss every relay in volleyball and my team hates me. In math, we have a pop quiz. I switch with Booger-Face for grading. He gets an eight. I get a four. Out of ten. Then my locker gets stuck and I can't get my stuff out. I mean really stuck. Looks like someone smashed a basketball against the door. Takes forever for the maintenance guy to pop it open with a crowbar. By then I've missed the bus home.

"You want a ride?" Mr. Corcoran, my English teacher, asks when he sees me watching the back end of my bus disappear down Palmetto Street.

"Yeah, OK."

I like Mr. Corcoran. And Mom's let him drive me home from detention before. He's got an English accent, which is extra cool when you teach English. Plus he likes comics as much as I do. When he caught me reading my copy of *Wolverine #7* inside the school's copy of *Macbeth*, he said, "No reason to hide what you're reading in my class, Mick. Great literature takes many forms." Since then we've been talking about Wolverine and the Hero's Journey and Batman and what makes a tragedy. Who needs Shakespeare when you got X-Men?

"Come help me load some books into my car, and then we'll go."

I follow Mr. Corcoran back into the school. He's got two boxes of paperbacks. I take one and he takes the other. One of the covers on top says *The Long Goodbye*. "What're these books for?"

"They're pulp detective fiction," he says. "The eighth graders had a good time with them last unit. Got a bunch of them reading something past chapter two." He sighs and shakes his head. "Then the board caught wind, and now it's back to the classics. Going to be a rough autumn slogging through Steinbeck. The man is dull as a tin spoon." He opens the door with his hip and then leans against it so I can get through with my hands full of box.

I have to go sideways down the front stairs so I can see where to put my feet. Mr. Corcoran waits at the bottom. He's already started his white RAV4 with the auto-start button on his key ring.

"So what's pulp detective fiction?"

"Well, the pulp is the type of paper used to print them. It was cheap, so more people could afford to buy books and magazines. And the stories themselves moved away from simple whodunits, where the sleuth never fails, to a version where the villain might win, and *if* the villain loses, the detective who brings him down is tough, street smart, and deeply flawed." He sets the box down.

"What flaws does the detective have?"

The back hatch pops open. "Depends on the book. Often the detective is both bad and good. Uncovering the villain but rejecting society's laws, acting as judge and executioner. He's both brutal and kind. Insulting and honorable. A loser and a winner. A loner at heart." Mr. Corcoran sets his box inside the vehicle.

I drop the box I'm holding next to his. "What about the villain? What's he like?"

"Sometimes the bad guy is innocent, and it is the victim who is the guilty mastermind. Sometimes there's no moral difference between detective, villain, and victim. Hard-boiled."

"Hard-boiled? Like eggs?"

"Ha! No, that's another term for these types of stories. The tone of the books is harder and darker, which reflects the society of the time: the Great Depression, World War II. The stories are driven by action, violence—psychological and physical—with a final confrontation when the detective faces his enemy."

"Does he win? The detective?"

Mr. Corcoran hands me a book from the top of one of the boxes. "Find out for yourself. Door's open on your side."

I come around the passenger side, and something tumbles from behind the front tire, scurries under the guardrail, and then disappears into the tall grass beyond the chain-link fence.

"Whoa."

"What is it?"

"I don't know. Looked like a big rat was under your car. Or a possum. Definitely had a tail." I peer under Mr. Corcoran's car. "Doesn't look like there's any more."

"Probably hiding in the shade. Let's go." He hops in and I follow.

The car rumbles quietly as we pull away. I stare back across the field. Had to be an animal I saw. But the tail. The tail glistened like a fender in the sun.

"That animal under your car, I think it had something metal stuck on it."

"Might've gotten into some garbage. I've seen too many birds and turtles with plastic can holders tight around their bodies. I always cut them up before I throw them away."

"This didn't look like plastic. Looked like metal, silver and shiny."

"You want to go back and try to find him?"

We pick up speed along Sandpiper Lane, passing through all green lights.

"No, that's OK. I gotta get home for my little brother."

"Finley, right?"

We turn onto Thirty-Ninth way too fast.

"Whoa." I plant my feet into the floor.

"Sorry. I swear I pressed on the brake for that turn."

The Sandyhollow Condominiums whip by, and I grab on to the passenger door. "Mr. Corcoran?"

"Something's wrong. I . . . I can't slow down. The accelerator. I think it's stuck." He pumps the brake. We keep speeding along toward the Windy Vale intersection. "Mick, my phone's in my briefcase. Would you call 911?" he says all calm-like. Except his eyes are huge in his head.

Up ahead, the traffic light switches to yellow. I unhook my seatbelt and pull Mr. Corcoran's brief-case from the backseat. I slide the clasps and open the lid.

"Hang on," Mr. Corcoran says, too late for me to hang on to anything. He lays on the horn as we swerve our way through the red light. Principal Nuñez's mouth is frozen in an *O* as we nearly clip off the front bumper of his SUV.

Tires squeal and screech.

Voices shout.

My heart leaps against my chest, battering against

my ribs to get out.

Mr. Corcoran's knuckles turn white.

His briefcase flips on top of me. Papers, pens, and phone fly around me and pelt the seats and windows.

"Hang on," Mr. Corcoran says again, and this time I twist and wrap my arms around the back of my seat, clinging like a monkey.

We swing onto Amnesty Street wide and fast. The car leans for a minute. I'm sure we're gonna tip and roll. Then we straighten and all four tires grip the road again.

"There's a hill on Garden Grove. I'm gonna–" The squeak in his voice sends a bowling ball down my gullet to crash-land in my stomach.

We turn wide again, this time bouncing onto the curb. People scramble off the sidewalk and flatten against the laundromat. Mr. Corcoran steers us back to the street, but another car's four lengths ahead. We're gonna smash into the back of its red caboose like a trash compactor.

"Hang on!"

I wish he'd stop saying that. Hanging on is all I can do. His phone is somewhere under the seats, and if I let go to search for it, I'm gonna get my first flying lesson. Through a windshield.

Mr. Corcoran speeds up.

Speeds up?

We surge into the oncoming lane to pass the red car. But there's a white truck heading right for us.

"Ahhhh!" Mr. Corcoran says.

"Ahhhh!" I say.

Just when I'm sure I'm gonna end up the middle slice of a car-part sandwich, we squeeze through an impossibly tight opening between red car and white truck. Car horns scream behind us.

"Garden Grove!" I shout. "It's the next left. Up ahead. Left. Left. Left!"

"Hang on."

We turn, and the force rips me from the seat, flinging me against the passenger door. The window bashes my head. No. That's not right. Other way around. Head bashes window. Either way, I think I'm gonna puke.

The car climbs the hill of Garden Grove. Slowing, slowing, slowing. Yes! And then ... it rolls ... backward. Picking up speed again.

"No. No. No!" Mr. Corcoran turns the wheel sharp, and the back end of the car hops onto the curb. "Hook your seatbelt. Now!"

I stare out the rear window. A light pole. He's

steering us right into a light pole. I turn around and scramble into the seatbelt. Can't get the latch. Can't. Get. Got it!

"Hang—"

A boom roars through my head. I jerk against the belt and it hugs me tight, squeezing the air outta my lungs. We've stopped, but the front wheels are still spinning.

Mr. Corcoran grabs my arm, his face turning from white to pink to white. "You OK?"

"Don't know." And I honestly don't. I feel really dizzy. The world looks gray around the edges.

Sirens, flashing lights, faces, and voices surround the car. I lean my head back and close my eyes.

Lose an Ally

I TUCK MR. CORCORAN'S detective book into a drawer and stretch out on Finley's bed. Tonight I'm not allowed up top. I'm supposed to take it easy.

"Were you scared? Running through red lights and driving on the sidewalk? Sounds scary. And exciting. Like in the movies." His voice is muffled as if he's talking through his pillow.

I wonder if I sound like that to him when I'm talking from topside. "No, I wasn't scared." Sweat beads bust on the back of my neck thinking about Principal Nuñez's face and Mr. Corcoran pounding his foot on a brake that doesn't brake. But I don't tell Finley. I don't need him thinking I'm a wuss. "It was kinda like riding a coaster." That runs off the rails and barrels through town.

Scratch. Scritch. Scratch.

Scuttle. Scratch.

"What the heck is that?" I prop myself on my elbow. "Did you hear that?"

Finley hangs his head over the side. His hair flops into a curtain around his face. "Yeah. Sounds like Harry."

Harry was Finley's hamster. He used to like to escape into the walls and make friends with the cockroaches. Problem is, Harry's been buried in a margarine container under the big oak near Gibson Creek for almost a year.

"Mice?"

"Roaches."

Scuttle. Scratch.

I roll off the bed and crouch on the floor. The bump on my head throbs a little from moving too fast.

Finley slides down the ladder. "You OK?"

"Fine."

He presses his ear against the wall.

I pick the wall opposite and do the same.

Scuttle. Scritch. Scuttle.

"It's over here!"

"Over here, too." I slide my ear against the wall, tracking the sounds to the closet. "Hey, get your penlight. We'll look inside one of Harry's old holes."

Finley rummages in the top dresser drawer and pulls out the tiny flashlight Uncle George got him to replace the one we lost in Zombie Cave. Then he slips on his gym shoes.

"What're you putting those on for?" I flip the switch for the closet light and shove the dirty-clothes basket aside.

"You always tell me to 'cause we never know when we gotta run." He hands me the penlight and then unplugs his sock from Harry's hole.

I kneel and shine the light inside.

A bright red beam shoots outta the hole and sears my hand.

"OW!" I drop the penlight. The flesh between my pointer finger and thumb has an eraser-sized, perfectly round blister. "Jeez." Stinks like burned bacon. Smarts, too.

Finley grabs the penlight.

"No. Don't shine it in there." I don't want whatever lasered me to get him too.

Lasers. What on earth could be in our wall that shoots lasers? If Finley weren't my witness, and if I didn't have a throbbing blister staring back at me, I'd think my bumped brain was playing a game of Hallucinate This.

"They're on the move again." Finley dashes out of the room and I follow.

Mine and Finley's school pictures rattle on the wall

in the hallway.

"Mom's room."

But the sounds don't stop there. They swing over the doorframe and scurry along the other side of the hallway. The overhead light flickers.

"What are they?" Finley cries out.

"Calm down." I start to bark orders to him 'cause that always helps distract him. "Go to the kitchen. Turn on the lights." I meet him by the sink and fling open the cabinet underneath. "Unplug Harry's fridge hole."

The fire extinguisher hangs on the inside wall of the cabinet, and I pull it off its hook.

Finley squeezes his hand in the gap between the baseboard and the fridge. Out pops the sock. "Help me move it."

We both yank on the fridge. I set the extinguisher down to get a two-handed grip. The blister on my hand stings. I try to ignore it. Tug and pull. Tug and pull. The fridge inches away from the wall so we can get better access to Harry's hole.

I pick up the extinguisher again and aim it.

Finley snatches the broom and jams it, stick side down, into the hole. "Haiyah!" The broom handle starts zigzagging back and forth. "Mick?" Finley hangs on, but now his arms are rocketing side to side like they're gonna get ripped from their sockets.

"Let go. Let go!"

Finley does what I said, and the momentum sends him reeling across the kitchen floor.

That's when the metal scorpion scuttles out of the hole after him.

Finley scrambles backward like a spider crab. The scorpion-thing advances on spindly-quick metal legs, pincers gleaming above its head.

Snap. Click. Snap.

Oly moly, the pincers are made outta needle-nose pliers, sharp, like blades. And the tail—the tail arcs and whirs, the tip a cutting drill bit.

"Mick?"

Finley's voice chops through my frozen brain. I pull the pin on the fire extinguisher and aim the nozzle, squeezing the handle tight, just as the scorpion-thing shoots a red laser at my little brother.

He screams, but I can't tell if it's a hurt scream from the laser or a scared scream from the foam shooting everywhere. Looks like a blizzard barreled through the kitchen. The scorpion-thing sizzles and sparks. I empty the extinguisher on top of it until all I see is a foam lump.

Finley's got his shoe off, rubbing the bottom of his foot.

I slip and slide next to him. "Let me see."

He holds his foot out for me. There's a pink spot on the ball. I pick up his shoe and stare into the hole singed through the sole.

"We can put ice on your foot till the sting goes away." Makes me think of the sting on my hand. Good thing Finley thought to slip his shoes on.

The broom peeks at me from under the slimy mess on the floor. I use it to prod at the scorpion-thing.

Nothing happens.

I reach down to grab it.

"Careful."

"I know. Stay there." I pull it up by its tail, which feels like a bicycle chain, except tiny wires are strung through the links. They attach to a tiny rotating motor, like from a model airplane, coupled to the drill bit. "This is some crazy stuff here."

"It's a robot." Finley stands and takes a closer look.

"Yeah. And a better model than the last one, that's for sure." The center of the scorpion is made from a computer mouse with an opening front and center. "The laser comes outta here."

"You think it's another scout? Like the last one?

To check out all the apartments before the bad guys rob everyone?"

"Must be. Someone must really have it in for Mr. Fouler. Searching his buildings and his tenants."

"There's more than one, Mick. We heard 'em in the walls. Where'd they go? You think they're at the neighbors' now?"

"Don't know. Maybe they got scared off."

"What if they come back? I don't wanna sleep here."

"I'll keep watch."

"But we don't have another fire extinguisher. I wanna sleep with Bagel Boy." He looks at me with his round, little-kid eyes, holding his shoe with the burn hole in the bottom.

"Yeah, OK. Get our pillows." I toss the robot in the sink and then stuff some ice in small plastic bags. One for Finley's foot and one for my hand. I'll have to come back, once Finley's settled in the shed with the dog, so I can mop up the mess before Mom gets home.

Finley joins me at the door, a pillow tucked under each arm. We lock up behind us and walk silently through the hall, down the stairs, and out the back.

The shed is a dark hulk in the moonless night.

"Got your penlight?"

Finley clicks it on and shines a weakly lit path. I can tell something's wrong the minute we get to the doorway. I fumble for the switch by the door and flick it, bathing the shed in light.

Tools are spilled out and scattered across the floor. Mr. Fouler's toolbox lies on its side, cracked open like someone put a chainsaw through it. The lawnmower's overturned and the blade and motor assembly are gone. Cans of paint have been squeezed in the centers like toothpaste tubes, lids popped off and paint smeared everywhere: blue, brown, gray. Where the dog's blanket used to be is a pile of shredded scraps.

I stoop by a patch of fuzz. Scared to touch it, I touch it anyway.

Dog hair. Sticky. With blood.

Finley drops to his knees and screams.

Admit Mistakes

WHEN MR. FOULER saw his shed, he wouldn't let Mr. Garnet call the police 'cause he didn't want them pawing through his stuff and "asking a lot of questions ain't nobody's business." He wouldn't even listen to me and Finley about the robots and the robbers coming. Instead, he blamed the dog for the mess, and me and Mr. Garnet cleaned it up best we could. Since Mom came home early after Finley called and finally got a hold of her at work, she handled the kitchen. Mrs. Garnet handled the weepy twins.

And the robot I sprayed with the fire extinguisher? Gone. Nothing but a glop of foam left in the sink. His buddies must've claimed him, or maybe he dried out and scurried off on his own six legs. Made it harder to convince mom there actually was a laser-shooting, metal-scorpion-robot scout in her home and not just me and Finley experimenting with fire response tools. But she came around once I showed her the blister on my hand and the hole in Finley's shoe.

She was so riled she took the last of our cookie jar money and went with Mr. Garnet to buy another lock at the twenty-four-hour Walmart. He bought one too and then installed both ours and his. By morning our door looked like we really do have something valuable to protect.

At breakfast Mom reapplied antibiotic ointment to my blister. She had to wrap my hand in a roll of gauze to keep the Band-Aid from slipping. Now I look like half my hand got chewed off. The thing itches, too, but only when I think about it.

Like now.

Under my desk, I tear off the medical tape and unravel the gauze until I have a twisty lump balled in my fist. The Band-Aid slides off in the mess. Much better. I stuff the used wrappings into my pocket.

"Stop calling me that, you idiot Neanderthal." Savannah's voice pierces my eardrums and I snap to attention. Yep, Van Demon is back at school.

"Savannah Diamond, there is no reason for shouting in my class. And there is certainly no excuse for name-calling." Mrs. Shumaker writes on her pink pad and tears a slip, dangling it in the air. "Take this to Principal Nuñez after class."

Savannah rises from her desk.

"And remove your hat at once. You know I don't allow hats in my class."

Now she notices? Savannah came to school wearing a pink baseball cap and hasn't taken it off all morning, far as I can tell.

"But . . ." Savannah bounces her gaze from face to face.

"At once."

She reaches up and tugs off her cap.

I expect her long blonde hair to fly out, or at least a ponytail to spring loose. Her hair does fly, but when it settles around her head, we all see it's sheared off before it even touches her shoulders.

"Oh, you cut off your hair," Marissa says. "It used to be so pretty."

"I prefer it short." Savannah glides down the aisle between a row of desks, her hat in one hand, the other outstretched for Mrs. Shumaker's slip.

"Less hair for the cooties." Xavier Johnson snorts when he laughs.

"Shut up, imbecile."

I don't know what imbecile means, but it sounds bad. And judging from the look on Mrs. Shumaker's face, it is really bad.

"Savannah, you will take *this* slip to Principal

Nuñez *now*."

Savannah plants her hat back on her head, grabs her notebook and pencil case off her desk, and stomps to the front of the room to claim her second pink slip in less than a minute. A new school record. I hold the old one: two in two minutes from Mrs. Salneck. It's a record I don't mind losing.

A pencil Savannah missed slides off her desk, bounces off her chair, and rolls across the floor. The pointy end aims right at me.

❖ ❖ ❖

Everywhere I turn, kids are talking about Savannah: How she cut her hair off 'cause of the lice. How her big words got her in big trouble. How Colby Holcum had to go home today because she got lice and everyone's sure Savannah's the one brought them back to school. Lice Girl this and Lice Girl that.

At lunch, I pour my milk into Booger-Face's lap. In science, I throw baking soda on Marissa Manning's notes and get my own pink slip. In gym, I'm the last one standing in dodge ball and Neill Gillis has a welt on his cheek the size of a—well, a dodge ball. And in between last bell and catching my bus, I hand Savannah her pointy, accusing pencil.

"Here." I thrust that snitch pencil in front of her face. "I'm sorry, all right? Sorry. Sorry. Sorry. Sorry. Just tell on me and get it over with."

She takes the pencil and examines it. "This isn't mine. I borrowed it from Josiah 'cause I left my number twos in my locker. But thanks anyway. Now I can give it back to him."

Not her pencil. Figures. "You heard me say I'm sorry, right?"

"Yeah. I heard."

"Well? What're you gonna do about it?"

"Um. I—" She takes a scrap of paper from the pocket of her backpack and scribbles on it with Josiah's pencil. A wisp of her shortened hair curls out from under her cap. It might as well point at me, too.

"What? It's so bad you can't say it? You gotta write it down? You want me to sign a confession?" Savannah's never at a loss for words. Why isn't she ranting at me? Yelling? Calling me three-syllable names?

"No. I . . . I have to tell you . . ." She sighs and looks me straight in the face with her blue-green, gold-flecked eyes. "I'm sorry too."

"You're what?"

"I'm sorry. I shouldn't have done what I did. I was mad and I overreacted. I hope you can forgive me. It got out of control. Not what I planned at all."

She's gotta be joking. Why else would she be saying what I should be saying? But part of me knows she's completely serious, 'cause look at how her eyes are all glossy like she's got tears ready to bust out.

"What did you do?" My voice comes out hoarse and quiet.

"I can't tell you here." She pushes the paper into the hand I got curled around the strap of my backpack. She slams her locker and dashes off. Her pink baseball cap bobs around the corner and she's gone.

I unfold the crinkled note.

She gave me her phone number.

Meet the Enemy

SAVANNAH'S NUMBER stares back at me from the kitchen table as I wait for Finley to get home from school. He shuffles through the front door. I listen for the drop of his backpack and the double clomp of his shoes releasing from his feet.

He pours himself a glass of orange juice and squeezes into a chair across from me without pulling it out from the table. His red-rimmed eyes tell me he's been crying about the dog again. I hope he waited until he was off the bus or, even better, inside the building. Tears are a bull's-eye on a boy's back.

"You look bad," I tell him.

"You look worse."

I straighten my hair with my fingers, then figure I don't care what I look like and turn straightening into a good scuff-scrub mohawk. "I apologized to Savannah today."

"That's good." He scans my face like he's trying to

read me. "She take it bad?" He sips his juice, eyeballing me over the glass rim.

"She got weird. I mean, weirder than usual. She apologized to me."

"What for?"

"Don't know. But she gave me this." I push the paper scrap closer to him. It's good we can be allies again. Teaming up with Finley feels like I got my arm sewed back on.

He finishes the last slug of his juice, wipes the wet off his face with his sleeve, and picks up the paper. "Her number. Wow. I sure wish she'd given this to me." His cheeks pink up like he got a sudden fever, and I try not to roll my eyes. "Wow," he says again. "Why'd she give it to you. She wanna yell at you over the phone?"

"That's the really weird part. She didn't seem like she wanted to yell at me at all."

"Well you should call her. And if she yells or cries, you gotta take it. And if she wants you to be her personal slave, you gotta do it." He pushes himself away from the table and sets his glass in the sink. "You"—he points at me—"gotta make it up to her."

Chastised by my little brother. Great.

Before I can tell Finley, "I know, I know," a howl

wrenches my words away.

Finley leaps to the window and pulls the curtain aside. "Bagel Boy!"

"Where? Is he out there?" My chair clatters, upended.

"I don't see him."

The howl starts again, loud and long and horrible, echoing through the room, wrapping around us like a coat of sad.

"That sound's in here, not outside." I set the chair upright and start to circle the table. "Something's not right. That howl's not right."

"The walls!" Finley grabs the refrigerator, yanking on it like a crazy kid. "He's in the walls."

"Think, Finley. He wouldn't fit." The dog is not a Chihuahua. I press my hands into his shoulders. "It's not real. Listen careful."

The howl repeats. Exactly like the first. Exactly.

"It's . . . it's . . . a recording?" His shoulders slump beneath my fingers.

"The robots."

His eyes widen in shock and then narrow with understanding. "The robots," he snarls.

"They're trying to scare us!" I shout the words. "But we're not scared, are we?"

"No way!" Finley yells. "I killed a zombie pirate. Twice. I'm not afraid!"

"That's right."

The scurry-scraping inside our walls sends an army of shivers marching down my back. The sound is louder than last night. Much louder.

"We have to go," Finley whispers. "Please." He stuffs Savannah's number into his shorts pocket.

We turn our backs together, facing out the way Uncle George taught us, to protect each other. Only when he taught us, we had wooden swords to fend off imaginary monsters.

These monsters are real, and made outta metal, and shoot lasers, and torture and kill dogs, and make sick recordings. And now there's gotta be a hundred of 'em crawling through our walls. Daylight doesn't reduce the creep factor, either. Somehow, it makes it worse.

Me and Finley inch toward the doorway. We need to slink to the hall, get our shoes, and sneak out the front door. Although a barefoot sprint to Mom at the grocery store is looking better every second.

Almost there. Almost there.

The wall above my head starts smoking, and a red beam pierces through the wallpaper from the inside out. Then the beam etches a fist-sized circle. Out pops the wallboard, followed by a metal spider with a cheese-grater head and a light-bulb belly. It twitches and glows, scurrying up the wall.

Tip-tap, scratch.

Another pokes through the hole and climbs after the first. This one's head spins, its face the blades from a blender, sparking and grinding as it clings to the wall.

Then another comes out. And another.

More and more holes are burned through our walls. Five or six behind us in the kitchen, four in the entrance hall, one to the left of the doorknob. Robots spill out: spiders, scorpions, giant ants, beetles, roaches, and centipedes. Made out of parts and pieces of work tools, kitchen utensils, bike parts, and electronic toys. Pieces soldered together onto tiny motors, wires strung like veins, their legs and claws and teeth sharpened into knife points.

I was wrong. There's not a hundred. I lost count after a hundred. They grip the walls, the molding, and the furniture.

Click, whir, scuttle, scrape.

Me and Finley are surrounded. If they all shoot their lasers now, we'll be sliced up fajita-style. They pour onto the floor in front of the door, scrambling toward us. We have to back away.

It's what they want. They've cleared a path behind us, wide enough for us to retreat, pushing us back into the kitchen and away from our exit.

I reach for the cabinet under the sink, hoping Mom or Mr. Fouler had a chance to replace the fire extinguisher. A scorpion shoots a laser from its tail and just misses my fingers.

My pulse pounds in the wound from last night, reminding me how much those laser beams hurt. I keep my hands to myself.

"The door locks. Listen. They're opening. Mom. Mom!" Finley dives forward, but I block him before he gets to the mass of robots in the entranceway.

"She's not due back yet."

"Who is it then? Mr. Fouler?"

Mr. Fouler does have keys to the place, but he's usually fishing at the docks until at least 6:00 p.m. And there's a new lock. Did Mom give him the key to that one yet? She wouldn't have had time.

The sound coming from behind the door doesn't give me warm fuzzies. Metal raking against metal in a world-record-breaking chalkboard squeal.

"It's more of them." Finley collapses into my arms

and buries his face in my neck. "What do they want? Why're they here?" he moans.

"We can't give up." I give him a little shake. I can't bear to tell him I think the thing behind the door is bigger than the ones that have us surrounded. The sound is bigger.

The new lock turns over. The front door's hinges creak.

The robots crawling on the floor, walls, countertops, and table hush and get still.

Finley peers around me. I can't help myself either. I turn to face what's coming, standing beside my brother.

Clomp. Clomp. Clomp. Clomp.

Metal hooves on linoleum.

R—iiiiiiiiiiip.

Metal claws through wallboard.

Clink. Clink.

Metal joints rubbing.

It rounds the corner and pauses in the kitchen doorway.

Finley gasps.

The same robot the dog had pinned in the shed, the one that got away, glares with burning eyes.

Except it's not. It's like when you take a beater

car in for a makeover and it comes back with a spiffy new paint job, rechromed bumpers, and an over-hauled engine. The same, but not the same. Better.

The cell phone inside its head crackles to life. "Are you scared yet?" a girl's voice sneers at us from the waist-high robot. The claw hands tighten and release menacingly. "Mickey Bogerman—are you scared now?"

The robot called me Mickey? My mouth feels like sandpaper. The wheels in my brain turn and my thoughts line up like pencils in a case.

There's only two people in the whole world that call me Mickey. One is my mom.

And . . . I know that voice. I should've recognized it when she said "retreat" in the shed. It's the same voice that called Xavier an imbecile today.

It's just like Mr. Corcoran said happens in those pulp detective novels when the victim isn't innocent after all. The victim is the villain.

Savannah Diamond.

Inflict Casualties

"NO. I AM NOT AFRAID of you." What is that girl playing at? Is this what she was sorry for? Setting an army of killer robots after me and my family because I put a couple bugs in her hair is not just overkill, it's nutzoid crazy sick. "If you can hear me, Savannah Demon, I do not accept your apology."

"Then fear this!"

A whine grows into a rumble, and before I can tell myself to keep my mouth shut, the robot shoots a fiery baseball outta its chest and clear across the room, blazing through the fridge, leaving behind a cavernous, smoking hole.

"Run! Mom's room, quick."

For the first time in our lives, Finley runs faster than me. I swear his feet don't touch the floor. Mine do. I have to shuffle and kick and crunch dozens of insect robots from my path. Their metal bodies scrape and prick my calloused feet. A couple of 'em sear holes through my jeans with their laser beams.

I barely notice a scorched hole on my thigh, barely feel the sting on my flesh.

Finley's already in Mom's room, waving for me to hurry up. He soccer-kicks a robot ant the size of a cat away from the doorway and then grimaces at the cuts on his toes.

The little robot whines and rumbles from behind, and I know what's coming next. The heat from the fireball fills the hall as it barrels through the wall above my shoulder. Our family picture crashes to the floor, glass shattering. The paint blisters around the hole, black smoke pouring above my head and licking the ceiling.

Me and Finley slam Mom's door shut, blocking the smell of charred wallboard. I can't slow my heart no matter how slow I try to breathe. It keeps wanting to break open my chest and run, run, run away. I press my chest against the door. But this thin wood door will not block a fireball. We need a better game plan than hiding in Mom's room.

Finley's rummaging through her closet, flinging clothes, shoes, toys, and books into piles on the bed and floor. Mom's closet is one of the few off-limits spots in our apartment where she can hide future birthday presents and her personal stuff. Hard to believe what she can fit in there.

"What're you looking for?" I want to help. "Finley?"

He doesn't respond, completely focused on his search.

OK then, I'll think up a plan of my own if I can't be a part of his.

We're too high off the ground to escape through Mom's window. Maybe if we tied the sheets together and then tied an end to the bed frame we could use them to climb down. The mound on Mom's bed grows. Her comfy bed with the thick mattress.

I swipe Finley's heap of closet stuff aside, strip the comforter, and slide the mattress off the box spring. Pulling, tugging, and pushing, I finally position the mattress upright against the door. It's not much, but hopefully it will slow down a fireball or two.

Scuttle, scrape. Scratch.

But the mattress can't keep the bugs outta the walls.

"Found them!" Finley holds up two Blast Buster Water Guns. "Remember these?"

Mom took them away from us last summer 'cause we were shooting the neighbors from our bedroom window. Of course I remember. Got grounded from the Eclipse Comic Emporium for a whole month. I'd forgotten she'd stashed the guns in her off-limits closet.

"You are a genius."

Together we dash into Mom's bathroom. This one's only got a toilet and sink. The hallway bathroom's the one with a shower and tub. But a toilet and sink are all we need to fill our guns. I lift off the back cover of the toilet. Finley gets the faucet going.

Scritch, scritch, scratch.

"Hurry." He tries to cram the water gun underneath the faucet.

"I'm hurrying. You hurry."

He can't fit the gun's fill opening under the water stream. The faucet's too low.

I hand him mine. "Here. Switch." The toilet tank's filling up. There's plenty of easy access water. It's a good thing, too.

The robots are breaking through the walls in Mom's bedroom.

"Haiyah!" Finley doesn't waste any time. He's pumping and shooting. A stream of water splats against a spider robot crawling out of a hole above the headboard. The bug sizzles, sparks, then scrapes down the wall and flops onto the box spring. Eight spiky legs spasm and then go still.

I join him and shoot at a centipede that's already hugging the floor. I can't quite get my target 'cause it's moving so fast. It snakes toward me, but once that bugger hits the puddle I made, it twitches, sputters, and dies. I aim for a scorpion just as it laser-shoots a pea-sized hole through Mom's stuffed rocking chair. That chair was me and Finley's go-to spot when we were little. Seeing the charred, smoking hole makes my blood thunder through my veins.

"Aaaagh!" I rush forward and drench that stupid mechanical scorpion. The light fades from its head and puffs out with a spark and a swirl of smoke.

"I need more water."

"I'll cover you." As Finley retreats to the bathroom, I squirt a roach, another centipede, and a robot that looks like a flat tick before it sucks blood. Then I'm outta water too.

"Ready." Finley appears by my side, his eyes narrowed and his lips tight. Looks like he's ready to kick some bug. "Go fill up. I got this."

I leave him for the bathroom. A spider's poised on the edge of the sink, mandibles clinking together like a wrench. Wait a minute. Its mandibles are a wrench.

Sweeping the barrel of the water gun across the spider's back, I knock it into the toilet bowl. It tries to scramble up the sides, but its legs can't hold on and it keeps slipping under the water. The ugly sucker makes a high-pitched squeal that twists my nerves into a knot before it twirls and sinks to the bottom of the bowl.

It's too big to flush, so I slam the lid shut and then kneel on it while I fill my gun from the tank. Just in case the robot's faking death and it tries to get out.

"Mick?"

Muscles tense, I join Finley. "I'm here."

"They're gone."

He's right. Only the dead or dying ones are left. I listen for scurrying in the walls. Only my heart and Finley's breaths sound in my ears. "Where'd they go?"

"They stopped coming. You think we got 'em all?"

I count eighteen bodies, not including the spider in the toilet. "No way. They could be waiting outside the door."

"But the sounds are gone. Let's look." He pushes on the mattress propped against the door.

"Let me do that. And let me look." The water gun's given him superhero confidence without the super powers. I gotta make sure he's not walking into a trap.

Once the mattress is pushed away, I crack open the door and peek. Nothing in the hallway but the broken picture on the floor and scorched hole in the wall. "OK, stay behind me." I keep the door partially closed, and we scooch out of Mom's room, inching down the hallway, water guns in our hands.

When we round the corner into the kitchen, my throat closes tight. Written on the wall in blood are these words:

FEAR US Mickey Bogerman OR ELSE

Follow the Trail

"BARBECUE SAUCE." Not blood. I pull the tip of my index finger outta my mouth.

"You think they just want to scare you? Maybe if you tell them you're scared they'll leave us alone." Finley wipes at the message with a washcloth, smearing the words into a big red swirl.

If only it were that easy. "There's no one here to tell but you. But next time I see psycho robot kid, I'll make sure to let it know its minions have made me almost pee my pants a zillion times already."

Finley sets the washcloth on the table and pulls Savannah's phone number from his shorts pocket. "You gotta call her."

"I'm not calling her." I tug open the drawer that's got the school directory, thumbing through the pages till I get to *D* for Diamond. There they are: 1212 Driftwood Drive. That's over by Gibson Creek. It'll take us a half-hour walk. Hopefully that will be enough time for the volcano of mad inside of me to cool off.

I write a note on Mom's notepad explaining what happened to the apartment, where me and Finley are going, and why. She'll be freaked for sure. But if we wait for her to get home to explain things in person, she won't let us out of her sight. She'll get involved. I don't want her to be those robots' next target. The last thing I write is for her to go stay with the Garnets. In case the robots come back.

Finley hands me my shoes. It's good to know he's on board.

"Let's go end this." I pat his back. "We'll take the guns."

Finley closes the front door behind us, and I turn the keys in the locks out of habit, even though robot kid can pick them.

Mrs. Garnet jogs down the hall after us. "Mick! Finley!" She raises her eyebrows when she sees our water guns. "Have you seen the girls? I was on the phone, and one minute they were watching TV, and the next minute they were gone."

Her phone conversation surely went past a minute, but I don't say that. "Did ya' look outside?"

"They always let me know where they're going, but they didn't even say they were leaving. But yes,

I checked outside, the shed, the laundry room, the dumbwaiter—everywhere."

Anyone under five foot tall likes to play in the dumbwaiter. Even Harry the hamster. Technically it's a little service elevator that used to bring packages up. It's been stuck on our floor ever since I can remember. Me and Finley got grounded more than a few times for hiding inside it. It was smart Mrs. Garnet checked there.

"Um, I'd help you look, but I got somewhere I need to be."

Finley steps forward. "I'll stay and help you, Mrs. Garnet."

"Thank you. I appreciate it, sweetheart." She looks so relieved I can't force Finley to come with me.

I nod so Finley knows it's OK. "Keep your gun with you." I dash down the stairs and out of the building.

That's when I see the trampled grass . . . and the tracks. Looks like a herd of animals crossed through the courtyard. Or an army of robots. A trail of dirt crosses the parking lot and then the street. How'd Mrs. Garnet miss this? She must've looked for her daughters before the robots made their escape.

I can't help myself, I have to follow. Their path could lead me right to the robots' secret lair. And if the twins saw this mess, they would've follow the trail too, or they could've followed the actual robots, or . . . gosh, that'd be crazy if those robots kidnapped Trish and Bridgett, and in daylight, too. No time to lose. I hug the water gun close to my chest and take off after them.

Only a block later, the dirt clumps and grass tufts left behind on the road spread out and then disappear. I've lost the robot tracks. I stand on the side of Canal Road and spin a three-sixty hoping to find a clue so I can pick up their trail again. It's so quiet that if I listen hard, I might be able to hear them.

Bugs hum, birds squawk, and squirrels rustle, but no robot feet pitter-patter. That's when I realize why it's so quiet: there aren't any cars driving to cover up Mother Nature. Yes, there's cars parked in driveways and on the side of the road, but in the time it took me to get from my apartment building to Canal Road, I haven't seen a single car drive by. Must be some crazy coincidence, right?

A flash catches my attention. There in the drainage ditch I find a flattened piece of steel the size of a postage stamp. Another flash up ahead and another steel swatch. Then I find a small bolt. And then a silver spring. When I move my head side to side, I can see the glint in the sunshine: a trail of metal parts.

My heart thumps and my fingers gripping the water gun get clammy. Is this trail for me? I follow even though my stomach churns and my head says, "You know you're by yourself, right?"

I don't bother to pick up the scraps left for me; I pick up the pace, instead. The trail leads me along the canal that spills into Cat Tail Bay, but before I get to the rock beach, I have to make a sharp right and cross Woodbine Bridge. I pass a man who parked his van at the scenic overlook. He kicks his tire and curses. There's a huge gash in the tire wall, and the wheel rests flat on the ground. Any other time I might stop to help him find his spare, but not today, not right now.

When I'm on the other side of the bridge, looking back across the canal, I see a strange sight: all but two of the cars in the canal parking lot have their hoods popped open. People are flailing their arms, pointing their fingers at each other, digging around in their engines, and generally acting crazy. Three guys circle motorcycles that from here look like all of their tires are blown out.

And the roads running alongside the canal are empty of drivers.

Something is very wrong here.

Whoa. I drop the water gun and squat in the gravel, my elbows on my knees. Might as well palm-thump my forehead. Finley would've figured it out a lot sooner. Knowing I figured it out for myself doesn't make it any easier to swallow.

The robots are putting a whole mess of cars out of order. It must've been one of the bug robots that jammed my locker and then messed with Mr. Corcoran's car. And now they're sabotaging all the cars in Beachwood. Maybe they're destroying the whole town's means of escape.

My temple throbs. I sink to my knees, pounding my fists. "You are truly evil, Savannah!" I shout to the sky.

Instead of an answer, I get more bad news.

Dangling above my head from a tree branch is Trish's sparkly, pink gym shoe.

STEP 12

Find the Lair

"TRISH? BRIDGETT?" I scan the trees and the canal. I run alongside the road and back again. Nothing. No more shoes. No girls. No scrap metal parts shining in the sun. The trail is cold.

The branches sway in the breeze, and the pink shoe twists this way and that. I set down my gun and then knock at the shoe with a stick until it tumbles to the ground. Then I tie its shoelace to the belt loop on my jeans.

I don't get it. Why did the robots want me to stop here? I poke the stick at the gravel, the grass, the leaves, and turn up more of nothing. I lean against the guardrail, not sure what I'm looking for, but I keep looking anyway. Stretching out over the railing, I see the edge of a large cylinder jutting from the earth. I climb over and then slip-slide down the steep hill, grabbing at roots and rocks, scrambling to slow myself until my feet land solidly on the top of a concrete drainage pipe.

The pipe is large enough for me to enter if I crawl on my hands and knees. I sit on the ground and scoot until I'm in position, then I pull myself onto the pipe's bottom lip. It's dry as a bone inside since it hasn't rained in Beachwood for a couple weeks. I peer into the darkness.

"Hello?"

Lo—lo—lo. My voice echoes back.

Scurry, scrape.

They're here, all right.

"Trish?"

Ii—ii—ish.

Scuttle. Scrape.

I poise at the entrance, ready to follow the noise, but then I stop myself. What would a hard-boiled detective do? He'd analyze the situation, of course. Think first, then act. If the girls were here, they'd be yelling their heads off. They're not exactly quiet kids. Plus, how would they've gotten in here? Robots couldn't have carried them down the hill. I could barely get down here myself without slipping into the canal.

Did they fall into the canal? I can't let my imagination go there. Besides, all the folks in the parking lot across from the canal would've done something about two little girls caught in the canal. No, they've got to be someplace else and the shoe . . . the shoe is a plant. A false clue to get me down here. These robots are playing cat and mouse with me. I will not be their mouse.

First off, it's dark inside the pipe—cave dark—and I don't have a flashlight. I've been in cave dark without a light before, and I'm not doing that again. Secondly, if I was a little robot with a horde of rat-sized bug robots and I wanted to ambush a kid, a pipe would be a good place. This pipe might as well have a banner with the word "TRAP" strung across the entrance. The third reason is kinda gross, but it sticks in my brain and propels my body back up to the safety of the road: if I died inside that pipe, no one would ever find me until my bloated-rotting-corpse stink got so bad you could smell it from up here.

I brush the dirt off my jeans and push my finger through one of the laser holes. Although my hand feels fine now, the skin on my legs still aches where the robot bugs got me today. Getting seared and cut up into pieces is not the way I want to go out. No siree.

Shaking my head, I realize what's most important: I can't do this alone. I ball my hand into a fist. Van

Demon is the only one that can stop her crazy robots. I've got to get to her if I want to rescue Trish and Bridget.

Gibson Creek runs into the canal a block ahead. Driftwood Drive isn't far. I grab my gun and pat Trish's shoe. "Hang in there, kid. We'll find you and get you and your sister home soon."

❖ ❖ ❖

Savannah's dad looks like some actor guy I saw in a movie once. The actor played a genetically enhanced hit man. When Mr. Diamond answers the door, I step back in case he wants to throttle me. Luckily, I thought to stash Trish's shoe and the Blast Buster in the bushes. They wouldn't help with first impressions.

He recognizes me right off. How, I'm not sure. Maybe he tore through previous yearbooks with his daughter until she slammed her finger on my picture and screamed, "He's the one, Daddy. He's the one ruined my life!"

"Mickey." His voice has that you-must-be-up-to-no-good-if-you've-showed-up-on-my-doorstep tone.

"Mr. Diamond." I hold his gaze for as long as I can stand it, which is about five seconds, and then my shoes need some eyeball time so I look at them instead.

"Is Savannah expecting you?"

"No, sir. I . . ." Is that a split in the toe of my left shoe? "I need to talk to her."

"Come in." He steps aside so I can enter his house.

I pause 'cause I'll have to walk past him, and he could throw his leg into my path and send me sprawling. I scan his face to see if he wants to.

He's Mount Rushmore. With frost.

I hold my breath—no idea why, just seems like it's a good time to hold on to some oxygen—and walk into the Diamonds' living room.

"Who was at the door?" Savannah bounds down the stairs, her short hair flapping around her head. "Oh. Hi, Mick."

"He says he needs to talk to you." Mr. Diamond shuts the door and stands in front of it.

No escape now.

"Let's go to the basement. I need to talk to you too." She gestures for me to follow her and waits for me to step across her family's plush white carpet.

I notice Savannah's barefoot and her dad's wearing socks. My shoes leave crushed, dusty prints. Something else for them to hate about me.

"Who came to visit?" Mrs. Diamond bops into the room just as me and Savannah reach the basement door. "Oh." She looks me over. "You."

She's an older, taller version of Savannah, except she wears glasses. She's also wearing—yeah—socks.

"Mick and me will be downstairs." Savannah flicks on a stairwell light and closes the door behind us.

As I follow her down the stairs, Mrs. Diamond's muffled voice floats above me. "What is *he* doing here?" and "Who's going to clean this carpet?"

"You did tell your parents I apologized, right?"

"I told them." Savannah glances over her shoulder. "They want me to turn you in, but I'm not going to."

I'm about to shout at her that I know why she's not turning me in—it's 'cause she's afraid everyone will find out about her killer robot army—when the stairwell opens out into the basement and my jaw drops to my chest. "Whoa."

The basement is a giant workshop. Worktables line up along the walls. Power tools are anchored on pegboards. There's a half dozen tool chests, each as big as the one in Mr. Fouler's shed. There's a router, a table saw, a compressor, a grinding wheel, a soldering iron, a couple circuit boards, and an old computer with an oversized monitor. Shoot, there's even a paint booth in the corner. A paint booth! The place smells of sawdust and turpentine. Sunlight squeezes through four ground-level windows above my head, but mostly it's fluorescent lights hanging from the ceiling that illuminate every corner.

Savannah smiles at my awe. "Like it?"

"I thought your dad's a teacher."

"You're such a chauvinist pig, Mick. This isn't my dad's shop."

"Your mom?"

She rolls her eyes at me. "It's mine."

"All this is yours?" Honestly, I'm not skeptical 'cause she's a girl. It's 'cause she's a kid, for Pete's sake. What kid gets their own paint booth?

"Yes. My parents like to encourage my interests."

Her interests? I run my hand over a worktable, and my fingers close into a fist around a pencil-sized metal spring. Just like one of the springs left on the trail from the robot army. The robot army she created right here in her personal workshop. My breath seethes and churns inside my chest like lava. "Do they know your interests include killing dogs, destroying apartments, slashing tires, and kidnapping little girls?"

Uncover the Plot

INSTEAD OF DEFENDING herself, she plops on a stool and covers her face with her hands. "I . . . I didn't know it would go this far. I . . . I created . . . a monster." She looks up at me and sniffles. "You have to believe me."

I don't let her off the hook. "MonSTERS. Not monster. You created hundreds of robot-bug, laser-shooting, slice-n-dice monsters."

"Huh? No. No. Only one." She spins on the stool and starts typing feverishly at the computer's keyboard. "Look. Here's my original design. I named him Oscar."

Rotating on the screen is a 3-D diagram of the little robot that the Garnets' dog pinned inside the shed. A bike basket wraps around his torso like armor. He wears a metal colander—the kind Mom uses to drain spaghetti—as a helmet. He looks kinda cute in a dorky-robot way, especially when he doesn't have a dog standing on him.

"Where's the upgraded version? The one with the bazooka coming out of its chest?"

"I didn't make any weapons. This is what I made. Oscar." She taps the screen. "At my old school, I use to compete on a robotics team. We placed first all the time." She ventures a smile, but when I don't smile back, she starts explaining some more. "I was furious at you for getting me kicked out of school, and I remembered what you said at the comic store about killer robots, so I wanted to make a special robot just for you. I programmed him using an app I downloaded off the Internet. I changed some code here and there. Then I synchronized it to an old cell phone I wired inside his head so I could communicate with him using my phone. The camera in the phone let me see what he saw."

"The cell phone sent pictures back to you. Just like Finley thought."

"Your brother. He's a smart one. Anyway, I kept track of Oscar using the GPS. Look here." She uses the mouse to open folders on the screen, double-clicks on a file, and a map pops up. "This is where I sent him." Using a zoom icon, she shows me an aerial view of my apartment building. "After the dog attacked him, I gave him instructions to come back, but he went here instead." With the mouse, she traces a road to town and stops on the top of Miller's Automotive. "This is where I lost track of him. That was Wednesday night. I thought he might still be there. So yesterday I went to the auto shop, but I couldn't find him. I couldn't find anyone. The lady at the beach store next door said Miller's got robbed Wednesday night and now it's closed until the insurance settlement comes in. At first I thought whoever robbed the place maybe took Oscar."

My head feels like it's underwater. "Let me get this straight. You created a robot here in your basement and then sent it to my home? To do what exactly?"

"Well, I . . . I programmed him to scare you. That's all. Just to scare you. Like you scared me . . . with the lice. Once he completed his mission, he was supposed to come back to me." She shakes her head. "Oscar wasn't very frightening. The dog certainly wasn't scared of him, and neither were you. Through the phone I heard you laugh. The whole thing turned into an enormous embarrassment. So I told him to retreat." Her voice rises. "I told Oscar to abort his mission. I told him to come back here." She gestures to the room. "He never came back.

"But he did text me." She pulls open a drawer and

fishes out a cell phone.

"What?" Did she say what I think she said?

"I kept calling him, telling him to come home. I even tried to shut him down remotely." After a couple finger pats on the front of her phone, she turns the screen to me. "Last night, he sent me this."

Mission in Progress. Abort Sequence Denied.
Conclusion Imminent.

I stare at the words until they become a blurred streak. My spit disappears. "Um. What's 'Conclusion Imminent' mean?"

"I think he's still trying to scare you. I think he won't give up until you are . . . you know . . . terrified. I think he created his own plan to make it happen." She slips the phone from my hand and sets it on the table. "He's thinking for himself. And if there are more robots, helper robots, he must've made them." She locks eyes with me. "I'm so sorry."

I swallow. Nothing but Sahara Desert tumbles down my throat. "How is this possible?" My mouth clicks when I talk.

"I keep calling and texting, but he's cut off all communication. I tried locating him with the GPS, but he must've deactivated it. I even went back to the website I got the app from, thinking I could get someone from customer support. They're gone. All I get is a '404 page not found' error." She bangs her fist on the keyboard. "Oscar's gone rogue, and I can't fix it."

"He—it—hasn't just gone rogue. It's created an army. It's appointed itself their master. It's turned into a weapon." I clasp my elbows, suddenly cold *and* spitless. "That robot of yours killed a dog, Savannah. It's tried to kill me a couple times. It's kidnapped my neighbors. They're little girls. Finley and their mom are looking for them now. It won't be long before Mrs. Garnet calls the police."

"I don't know why this happened." She chokes back a sob and scrubs a tear across her cheek with her palm. "I only programmed him to scare you. Like boo-scare, not scared to death. I don't know what went wrong. It wasn't supposed to be like this."

Footsteps tromp down the basement stairs. Overly loud, so we know they're coming. "Mick? Your mother is on the phone." Mrs. Diamond climbs back up and closes the door with a click.

"There's a phone on the wall." Savannah points and then pulls a tissue out of a nearby box.

I pick up. "Hello?" I hear Mrs. Diamond click off. "Mom?"

"Mick, is your brother with you?" The worry in Mom's voice grabs at my heart.

I gulp. "No. I left him with Mrs. Garnet. To help her find the twins."

"Your note says he's with you. Do you know where he could've gone?"

"No, Mom." I feel myself shrinking into my shoes.

"Trish and Bridgett aren't home yet, and now your brother is missing, too. You know all his hideouts. I need you to come back right away and help me look for him." She doesn't even wait for a response before she hangs up.

"What's wrong?" Savannah stands next to me, eyes wide. "You look like you're gonna get sick."

No, not sick. The feeling in the bottom of my belly is the same one I felt when I was trying to escape from Zombie Cave. The same one I felt when a bloodthirsty mermaid swept me into her scaly arms. It takes me a minute to form words. When they finally come out, they shake and squeak.

"I'm scared."

Recruit the Troops

"WHY? WHAT HAPPENED?"

Savannah's sympathy is like a slap to my face. Snapping out of my panic, I slam the receiver back onto the phone. "Happy now? Your robot's got my brother."

"Oh no. I . . . I didn't know it would come to this."

I stare at Savannah hard. "You don't know. You don't know anything. I came here hoping you'd help, and you're no help at all." The stool I kick topples to the concrete floor with a bang.

"Mick, I can help. I know I can. I'll help put this right. I'll help find your brother and those girls." She picks up the stool and offers me a seat. "Please."

"I have to go look for him." I charge up the stairs.

Rummaging sounds and the slam of a drawer make me look back. Her backpack slung over her shoulder, Savannah races up the stairs behind me and grabs my arm. "Wait."

I shrug her off, throw open the basement door,

and stomp across the fluffy carpet. OK, muffled stomps, more like thumping. The deadbolt sticks when I try to open the front door, which gives Savannah a chance to catch up with me.

"Let me get my shoes. Mom!" she hollers. "I'm going to Mick's." She scrambles into some gym shoes and tumbles out the door after me.

Snatching Trish's shoe and the water gun from behind the bushes, I turn to face her. "If you're coming with"—I slap the side of my gun—"you have to bring your own weapon."

"I did." From a pocket on her backpack she pulls out a black rectangular casing, sorta looks like a fat video-game controller.

"What is it?"

"It's an EMP emitter." She sees my confusion and explains without my having to ask. "Electromagnetic pulse. It'll disable any electronic equipment within a couple feet. It's not that hard to make. The instructions are on the Internet: copper wire, an iron tube, the capacitor from a disposable camera. I stuck the workings inside this model airplane remote so I could hook it up to a switch."

Even my water gun looks more intimidating than her EMP thingy. "Will it take out Oscar?"

"It knocked out my mom's laptop—boy did I get in trouble—so yeah, it'll blast away the junctions in his semiconductors." She smiles at my raised eyebrows. "It'll stop Oscar in his tracks."

"All right." Having a brainiac on my side might be useful. "You can help."

She touches my arm again, and this time I let her keep her hand there. "If there's as many robots as you say, we're gonna need more than just the two of us. I'll only have one chance. The capacitor that triggers the EMP gets fried after one use. And I have to be close. The range is a foot or two. I'm sure you're a good shot, but one water gun isn't gonna disable all those other robots so I can get near Oscar."

Ugh. She's right. They've got numbers on their side. Me and my water gun will be overpowered. It's the reason I came looking for Savannah in the first place: I can't do this alone. But even the two of us together aren't enough against hundreds of robots.

"We've gotta get our own army." She pockets her EMP controller and exchanges it for a cell phone. "The calls better come from you. No one's gonna come help Lice Girl."

"Yeah. Um, sorry. That's not a name I picked out."

"Right, Van Demon is so much better."

"How'd you know about that?"

"You are talkative and predictable."

"Right. And I'm a chauvinist and an ignoramus. Well, you're a . . . you're a . . . big-word user." I tie off Trish's shoe again, but I can't hold my gun and the phone. We'll waste valuable time if I can't walk and talk, so I hand my gun off to Savannah.

She gives me her phone. "'Big-word user,' huh? Van Demon has more panache. If you're going to throw insults, stick with that one."

Great, now I gotta look up panache. Does this girl ever stop? "How do I call someone on this thing?" There are pages of apps to slide through; I can't find her contact list. Or how to get to her keypad.

"The numbers for everyone in our class are loaded off the school directory. Yeah, those days off from school freed up my time. Voice prompts are on. Just say the name of who you want to call and the phone will connect you."

"OK, let's go." Jogging, I start with Booger-Face. For a minute I forget his real name. "John MacDougal," I eventually say into Savannah's phone. It rings back at me until Booger-Face picks up.

"Who's this?" He sounds like his mouth's full.

"Hey, it's Mick."

"Hey, Mick. This isn't your home number. Where you calling from? Did you finally get a cell phone?"

"No, I'm borrowing a phone from . . . someone." I don't want to tell him about Savannah yet. I'll get sidetracked with explaining. "You got a water gun? Or a fire extinguisher?"

Savannah looks at me funny.

I mouth the words "long story."

"Yeah. What's up?"

"I need you to grab water guns, fire extinguishers, flashlights, whatever you've got, and meet me on the south side of the canal by Cat Tail Bay. You know where the parking lot is?"

"Yeah."

"Across Woodbine Bridge from that."

"I thought we were going to your place?" Savannah asks.

I put my finger across my lips to signal for her to be quiet. "Finley's not at my place," I whisper to her. "But I might know where he is." Then back to the phone I say louder, "And call Neill and Cooper for me. Have them come."

"And Marissa," Savannah whispers.

"And Marissa, too. Anybody you can get a hold of. But they gotta bring water guns. Or fire extinguishers.

Otherwise I don't want them there. OK?"

"OK, but what should I tell 'em we're gonna do?"

"Tell them . . . " I remember I'm talking to a kid. And he's gonna talk to other kids. It's not like talking to adults where I gotta twist the truth so it'll squeeze into a narrow adult mind. Booger-Face's brain can handle the facts. "We're gonna destroy a killer robot army."

He finishes chewing whatever he's chewing, and I hear him swallow. "Awesome."

Communicate the Plan

ME AND SAVANNAH arrive at the guardrail above the drainage pipe before anyone else. The sun is low enough in the sky that the trees cast spindly shadows across the gravel road. I hope Booger-Face remembers a flashlight. We're gonna need it just to climb down.

"This is where the trail ended and I found Trish's shoe, up in that tree. And down there is the pipe. I heard the robots inside."

Savannah stretches over the guardrail to get a better view. "Did you see them inside the pipe?"

"No, I heard them."

"How do you know it was them?" She pops back up, resting her legs against the railing. "Maybe it was an animal."

"Trust me. I know the sounds they make. It was them, all right." Nothing else in the world makes that metallic scraping noise. And nothing else rockets goose bumps down my spine in the same way.

"And those are the cars that were damaged?" She

points to the parking lot across the canal.

"Yeah." The cars and motorcycles are in the exact positions as when I left. Even the van on the bridge hasn't moved. No tow trucks have come, either. No police search for the vandals.

And no people. The place is deserted.

"OK. While we wait for the others, tell me more about the lasers." She plops on the ground and crosses her legs.

I join her, resting my gun across my lap. "I can tell you they hurt. Here and here"–I point to the holes in my jeans–"and here."

"Bet that automotive shop had a laser cutting or engraving tool. That might explain how Oscar gave his army laser capability. He doesn't want to kill or permanently maim you, though. The lasers aren't cutting through to your bone, just the first couple layers of clothes and skin."

"Nice to know."

"I worry that he'll do more damage to the person you care about."

"You mean Finley." That's what I'm worried about, too. I wish Booger-Face would get here soon. I strum my fingers along the plastic casing of the gun. The *tap-tap* sounds like *hur-ry, hur-ry*. I try to keep

Savannah talking so I don't go nutzoid. "You talk about that robot like it's a person, with motives."

"No, I know he's not. A person you can reason with. A person will look out for their own self-interest. Oscar's programmed with a single purpose; that's his motive, and he's gonna see it through even if it means he gets destroyed."

It's good we can agree on something. Oscar is not a person. He's a nasty little machine, and if he hurts my brother, I'm gonna tear him apart.

"I know how to stop the lasers." She unzips her backpack and pulls out a compact, like what my mom uses to check her face.

"What, you gonna throw makeup at them?"

"No, silly." She snaps off the lid and holds it out for me to see. "A mirror."

"Great idea." Wish I had thought of it.

She puts her backpack in front of her face and then peeks around it. "And we can use this as a shield."

Seeing her duck behind her backpack reminds me of when I broke into her locker, dug through that same backpack, and put the lice in her hairbrush. I have the urge to apologize for the millionth time. "I'm sorry you had to cut your hair."

"You think I cut my hair because of you?"

"Well, yeah. 'Cause of the bugs."

"I got it cut because I wanted short hair. And because I had more than ten inches cut off, I could donate my hair to Locks of Love. You know, the place that makes wigs for kids going through chemo. I wanted to cut it. I didn't have to cut it."

I don't know what to say. I should tell her what she did was really cool, but Booger-Face and a gang of kids are coming up the road dragging a noisy wagon covered in a sheet. We jump up and run to meet them.

Neill pulls the wagon, followed by Cooper and Booger-Face, and Marissa and Brendan trail behind, squirting each other with their guns.

"Save your water," I yell at them.

"We could only snag two fire extinguishers without getting caught, but we got six water guns, loaded and ready." Booger-Face rips the sheet off the wagon to show me the stash he's brought.

Cooper pulls out a tiny water pistol, the kind that holds a teacup full of water. "I brought my water gun."

Booger-Face snatches it and tosses it into the canal.

"Hey!"

"Cooper, you are a dork." Booger-Face thrusts a double-barreled Extreme Water Blaster 2000 into Cooper's arms. "This is a water gun."

"Hey, Savannah, didn't know you'd be here," Marissa says.

My friends might as well have a big question mark painted on each of their faces. Brendan's mouth hangs open like a Venus flytrap while his gaze darts from me to Savannah and back again.

I can't take time to explain how me and Savannah joined forces; instead I give them the details that matter. "The robots captured my brother and two little girls. Our job is to rescue them. We're gonna destroy the robot soldiers with the water guns and the fire extinguishers so Savannah can get close enough to knock out the lead robot with a magnetizer. The robots look like metal bugs the size of cats, they have sharp claws and stingers, and they shoot lasers, so you'll need to be careful. Conserve water. Aim for their heads and bellies. Take out as many as you can.

"The pipe's not big, so we gotta go in one at a time. I'll go in first and use Savannah's backpack as a shield. Then Neill, Cooper, Marissa, Brendan, and Savannah. Booger-Face, I need you to be last in case any come at us from behind. Any questions?"

"Lasers?" Marissa's eyes widen.

"Claws and stingers?" Brendan takes a step back. "No one said anything about us getting hurt."

"Shouldn't we let the police do this?" Marissa turns her water gun over in her hands. "They use real guns. They're trained."

"The time we take to convince adults to believe us is time Mick's brother doesn't have," Savannah says. "I know this robot, and he's not going to give up until his mission is complete. He's capable of anything." She puts her hand on Marissa's shoulder. "Look, I know you're scared. I'm scared too. But Mick and I . . . we can't do this by ourselves. We need your help, and we need to do this now."

"Count me in!" Booger-Face grabs a fire extinguisher from the wagon.

"I'm in," Cooper says, a water gun in each hand.

"Me too." Neill fist-bumps me. "Come on, Marissa. Don't be a wussy girl."

Marissa shrugs. "OK, I'll do it. But I want the other fire extinguisher. And my own flashlight."

"Well I'm not." Brendan throws down his water gun. "I think you're all stupid. Crawling into a pipe. Water guns against lasers. No way."

"Scaredy-cat," Booger-Face says with a snarl.

"No, it's OK," I say. "He's OK. Maybe you can stand here on the road. Shout out a warning if you see anything suspicious." I pick up his water gun and hand it back to him. "Or you can go home. Your choice."

His gaze darts to each of us and then rests on me. "I'm sorry. I'm gonna go home." He turns on his heel and jogs off.

"Hey! Leave the gun!" I shout at his back, but he doesn't turn around.

"Well, he's never gonna hear the end of this," Neill says.

We don't have time to worry about Brendan. "Let's go." I hurry back to the guardrail with my friends behind me.

Savannah pockets her EMP box and then helps me thread my arms into the straps of her backpack.

"It's easier to sit and slide so you don't pitch forward and tumble into the canal. Just get near the pipe. We can help each other get inside." I climb the guardrail first and scoot down on my backside. Next to the pipe's opening, I toss my gun inside and pull myself in after. Neill scrambles down, and I grab his arm to help him onto the lip of the pipe.

Neill helps Cooper inside. Then Marissa follows, Savannah next, and Booger-Face last. We're a noisy group, and it takes a few minutes to hear anything except ourselves. I listen hard for the scraping of metal on concrete.

"I hear something."

"Me too."

"Shh."

Ooowooo.

"What was that?"

"Turn on the flashlight."

Howoooo, owoo.

"There it is again. Hey, get your elbow outta my side."

Ow-ow-wowooo. Arf, arf. Arf, arf. Howoooo.

"Mick? Is it a robot?"

"No. It's a dog."

Locate the Prisoners

"IS IT THE SAME dog from the shed?" Savannah's voice echoes inside the pipe.

"Sounds just like him. But it could be a recording again." Everyone is pin-drop quiet while I talk. "Last time I heard the dog howling it was the robots playing a recording of him getting tortured. Me and Finley could tell it was a recording 'cause the same howl looped again and again."

"That's sick." Shadows from the flashlight make Booger-Face's face into a frowning mask.

"Why would they play it now? Are they trying to scare us?" Marissa clutches the fire extinguisher close to her chest.

Now is no time for lies to make everyone feel better. "Yes," I tell her.

"We should follow the recording to its source," Savannah advises.

"Let's get the sicko robot dude!" Booger-Face pushes us forward.

We inch onward. It's slow going 'cause we're all carrying something. I push the backpack ahead of me with one hand, my other clasped around my water gun. Neill shines the flashlight over my shoulder. The beam bounces as he moves.

Owooo. Arf, arf.

The dog sounds closer now.

I expect a metal centipede or a spider to drop on top of me, pincers digging into the flesh on my back. I imagine a laser searing through Savannah's backpack and scorching my forehead. Any minute my friends are gonna start screaming as robot bugs encircle us, cutting off our escape routes.

But all I feel are my jeans rubbing against my knees. All I see is more empty pipe ahead. All I hear are the sounds of my friends crawling, their short breaths, the occasional scrape of a plastic gun, and the dog's howls getting closer.

There's something I haven't told anyone yet. Something kinda important. The howls we're tracking don't sound the same as what I heard in my apartment. They don't sound like a recording at all.

"Look, there's light up ahead." Neill wiggles the flashlight more than usual. "See? There's an opening to the sky. Maybe we can get out that way?"

"Or the robots can get in," Marissa says from behind me.

"Keep going. We'll see when we get there." At least no one's talking about turning around. I have a lot of respect for them backing me up. I hope we can end this quick so everyone can go back home.

When we get to the end of the pipe, it's me who wants to turn around.

The pipe opens into a ginormous vertical tube and then continues on the opposite side. At the top is a circular metal grate that lets in the light, and water if there was some. The tube looks like it runs straight down through the center of the earth and back out to China. Metal rungs are imbedded in the concrete: a ladder, but on the opposite side of the tube.

About ten feet down, strung across the tube and wrapped in fishing net, are ... people. Dozens of people.

I hold my hand up behind me and signal Neill to stop so he doesn't knock me outta the pipe. He sends the signal back to the rest of our group.

The light spilling through the grating makes square shadows across the frightened faces of the people below me. They don't scream 'cause their mouths are sealed shut with packing tape. They don't fight back 'cause their hands are taped, too. Bug robots swarm along the outside of the rope cocoon. Occasionally one of the robots zaps someone inside. A groan follows and the smell of burned skin.

The only struggle comes from Bagel Boy. He's pinned inside the net too, and now that he sees me, he barks like a maniac. The people crane their heads, their eyes widen at the sight of me, and for a second I just gape at them, my brain frozen.

I hold my finger to my lips even though the townspeople can't speak, 'cause if they start to struggle, they'll draw the robots' attention to me. They seem to understand and lie still while I scan each face and count. The guy with the van on the bridge is there. I sorta recognize the three motorcyclists tangled in a black leather heap. Twenty-seven, maybe twenty-eight all together. Not sure if those giant feet go with that blonde guy or not.

But no kids. My brother isn't with them. Neither are Trish and Bridgett.

"What's the holdup?" Booger-Face shouts.

"Shh!" Marissa screeches.

But it's too late.

"Robots!" Neill yells as metal bodies clamor into our pipe. While I duck behind the backpack, he drops the flashlight and shoots his water gun over my head. Only a tiny stream arcs from the nozzle.

"Pump it first. You gotta hit them hard. Go for their bellies."

A centipede tries to scurry past me, clinging to the pipe above me. I scrape the bug off with Savannah's backpack and fling it onto its back in front of me. Neill pumps his gun. He squirts the centipede's underbelly. A spark, a sizzle, and the squirmy legs stop squirming.

"What's going on?" Booger-Face hollers.

"What's happening?" Marissa joins in.

I've gotta tell them. They think we're here to rescue a few kids. They don't expect to rescue a bunch of adults, too. How're we gonna reach them? We can't just jump down and start cutting ropes; all of us could fall to our deaths. My instincts say turn. Save myself. My friends. I don't know those people. But my heart booms in my chest: *Save them—pound, pound—save them all.*

I need Savannah's help to figure this out.

Robots scurry into our pipe two to three at a time. Neill seems to have gotten the hang of taking them out. He sweeps his gun in a circle in front of us, completely silent and focused on the kill. Cooper's shooting through the space above Neill's shoulder, catching the ones that got missed. Robot bodies start to pile up. I leave the backpack shield for them and squeeze behind.

From back here the scrape and sizzle of robot carnage is muffled beneath Neill's and Cooper's grunting. It's darker back here, too. Marissa's got her flashlight pointed at the ground instead of pointing it at my face.

"The robots?" she whispers.

"Lots of 'em. Neill and Cooper are keeping them from getting back here. But there's something else."

"Spill it," Booger-Face demands.

"There are . . . people captured. In the pipe up ahead." I explain what I saw, describing the fishnet cocoon and the robot guards. "My neighbor's dog is there, too."

"You said he was dead."

"I thought he was. But he's not. Yet."

"There's got to be ropes holding the cocoon to keep it from falling. How're they attached to the pipe?" Savanna asks.

I try to remember. "One rope's tied to the ladder. A couple are tied to the edge of the grate–"

She interrupts. "Is there one close to us? Can you get to it?"

"Maybe. Probably."

"We can climb down that one until we're on top of the fishnet and slice an opening in the top of the cocoon. We can all climb up the ladder and go through the pipe on the other side."

"Not the dog," Booger-Face cuts in. "Dogs can't climb ladders."

He's right. Not even a circus dog can climb a ladder that goes straight up and down.

"We'll have to work together and hand him up." Savannah pauses, thinking. "Or use the cut ropes to tie around him and hoist him up."

"Um, guys? Guys?"

"That could work. Once the adults are free, they can help with the dog." Marissa taps her flashlight. "The adults will get us outta here."

I don't remind Marissa we're the ones saving the adults.

"Guys? I don't mean to break up your party, but we've got a problem." Booger-Face snatches Marissa's flashlight and shines it back the way we came.

Sneaking through the pipe, coming at us from behind: robot bugs. The gleam from hundreds of metal pincers flashes in the tunnel. We have no choice but to move away from them and toward the cocoon.

Initiate the Rescue

"MOVE. MOVE!" I scramble, trying to get around Cooper and Neill as Booger-Face opens the fire extinguisher on our pursuers. I leave behind Savannah, who's got her mirror out, deflecting the lasers getting past Booger-Face so they don't hit her and Marissa. At the front of the pipe, my gun's aimed and ready for the assault.

But the robots aren't there.

"Where'd they go?"

Neill points.

The robots that used to be attacking Neill and Cooper scurry across the net, their spindly legs poking at the people trapped inside the cocoon. More robots hang from the grating like bats in a cave.

"Hello, up there!" Booger-Face's voice rises through the pipe. "We're kinda trapped back here."

"We've gotta go."

"Go?" Cooper squeaks. "Go where?"

I feel below the lip of the pipe, and my fingers

close around a large knot anchored into the concrete tube with a metal eyebolt. I give the rope a tug. Seems sturdy. Must be, to hold a fisherman's catch of adults above an abyss. What's the weight of a few kids added to that?

"You want us to go in there?"

"I'm outta foam, guys," Booger-Face hollers from behind. "Guys?"

I stuff my water gun up the back of my T-shirt and knot the cotton tight around my waist. Not the most comfortable way to carry it, but I need both my hands free. I swing my legs outta the pipe and wrap them around the thick rope.

"What's he doing? Is he nuts?"

I block out the sounds of Cooper's worrying and Booger-Face's shouts and focus. Relax my legs, hand under hand, then contract my leg muscles. Relax, hand under hand, contract. I descend the rope toward the cocoon, the black void yawning below like a giant's throat.

Finally my feet touch the cocoon. I squat and release the rope. The robots skitter out of my way as I crawl along the fishing net. I try not to knee anyone in the face or crush anyone's fingers.

Neill is already down the rope. Cooper follows,

keeping his eyes closed and swearing like the guys at the docks. Any of those words came outta my mouth, I'd be tasting soap for a week, but I don't say anything. If that's what it takes for him to cope, that's what it takes. I'm no judge.

Savannah coaches Marissa down next and then follows. Booger-Face tosses the backpack, water guns, a couple flashlights, and the last fire extinguisher to Savannah and Marissa before he shimmies down the rope like a fireman.

The net sways with the extra weight of the six of us. Neill pulls out a folded knife from his pocket and waves it at me. I point to a spot on the cocoon close to the ladder, and he starts sawing.

All the while, the robots watch.

The dog is not watching. He's wiggling and howling.

Marissa crawls to him, petting him through the net, soothing him with baby talk. It seems to work.

"Hey, it's getting too dark to see. Someone shine a light over here. I don't want to cut someone."

Booger-Face crawls over to Neill and aims a flashlight on his work. Looks like he's almost through one rope link. It's slow going. Fishing net is tough stuff. He might cut an opening big enough for the people to escape before the sun leaves us with nothing but a couple flashlights in a barrel full of dark.

The robots chitter.

"Hurry, Neill."

"Another knife would be good." His elbow ratchets into a blur as he hacks at the net.

Booger-Face shakes the flashlight at Neill. "We didn't plan on cutting through rope."

"No, just battling robots with squirt guns."

"Hey, it works," I jump in to defend Booger-Face. The water guns were my brother's idea after all.

"Until we run outta water. Which Cooper and I did a couple minutes ago."

"Quit fighting," Marissa hisses. "Look up there."

At the top of the ladder, standing inside the pipe, Oscar glares down at me and grins.

OK, so he doesn't actually grin. But if he could, I bet he would, standing over us like a psycho king.

"What have you done with my brother?" I shout up at him, clasping the pink shoe still tied to my belt loop. "Where are Trish and Bridgett?"

"Are you scared yet, Mickey Bogerman?" The voice coming from the robot is Savannah's, but not Savannah's. Slower, deeper, emotionless.

I feel like my insides got scooped out with a giant metal spoon.

"Yes! OK? I'm terrified. You won. Now tell me where my brother is."

Outta the corner of my eye, I see Savannah approach the ladder. Her left hand stretches toward the first rung. The left wraps around her EMP box.

I keep talking, trying to distract Oscar to give her the time she needs to get close to him. "You won. I'm scared to death. You've captured all these people, my neighbors, my brother. There's nothing you can't do, and there's nothing I can do to stop you."

Savannah's only five rungs away now.

"I'm shaking in my shoes. All these robot bugs ready to attack me and my friends."

She's almost there.

"I've faced a lot of scary stuff and still wasn't as scared as I am now."

Oscar's body rumbles.

"No! Wait. What're you doing?"

"I don't believe you, Mickey Bogerman." The circle in the center of Oscar's chest glows orange.

"No, no, no!" This can't be happening.

"Savannah, watch out!" Booger-Face shouts.

She swings to the right, dangling from one rung as the fireball rockets down the ladder. The edge sears her hand. She screams, drops to the net, and curls into a ball, clutching her hand against her stomach.

The fireball scorches through one of the ropes suspending the cocoon, and the whole thing pitches forward. Marissa shrieks. The dog howls. People moan.

I drop to my belly and hug the net, scooching toward Savannah. "Are you OK? Let me see your hand."

The side of her wrist is bright red with blisters.

"Agh!" she cries. "Hurts bad. Real bad."

"You monster!"

Oscar disappears into the darkness of the pipe above. His minions click, chitter, and scrape as they follow.

"Go after him," Savannah says through clenched teeth.

"I can't leave you."

"He wants just you. That's why he got me out of the way."

"Hey, I've cut through the net. Someone help me get this guy out."

Cooper crawls over to Neill.

"Go," Savannah urges. "We'll catch up."

"OK, I'll go. Where's the EMP?"

She shakes her head, her blonde hair gray in the fading light. "I dropped it."

Try Not to Die

MY GUN SCRAPES against my back. I climb the ladder with one hand, a flashlight clasped in the other. Once I reach the lip of the pipe, I take one last glance over my shoulder.

Booger-Face squirts water from his gun onto Savannah's wrist. Marissa cuddles the dog, who's finally calmed down. Cooper and Neill pull tape off hands and mouths. The biker guys haul people out of the opening Neill made in the cocoon.

I have no choice. I follow the scuttling noise. The pipe goes on forever. Or maybe it just feels that way 'cause I'm alone. My palm is so slick with sweat I can hardly hang on to the flashlight, and when I try to keep my fingers from trembling, they shake even more. Oscar's wrong about me. He just doesn't recognize a puddle of wussy-kid when he sees it.

Every few feet there's a drainage tube over my head, and speckled moonlight spills through the openings. This pipe must run alongside a road. No traffic sounds, though, just the chirrup of crickets letting the world know it's nighttime. Then up ahead I hear voices. Soft and murmuring, like people are having a hushed conversation.

I pick up my pace but then slow down right before the pipe empties into a rectangular catch basin. A small grating lets in fresh air and some night sky so I can sorta see what's what. There, tucked into the farthest corner, next to a big pile of leaves and storm debris, are Finley, Bridgett, and Trish. They're not tied or taped up, either. They're sitting cross-legged around a flashlight, like they're gonna sing "Kumbaya" at camp.

There's not a robot in sight.

I wait a minute, searching for robot movements, eyes peeled for Oscar. When my heart retreats from my throat back into my chest, I figure it's time to make my presence known.

"Finley."

He turns to stare at me, and I see the smudges and scratches on his face. He's put up a fight. I push down my anger. I gotta be able to think clear to get us out of here.

"Mick! You've come to rescue us." Bridgett moves into the light. She's head-to-toe filthy, like she's been rolling in the mud.

Wherever the robots hide, they know I'm here now. I crawl from the pipe, put my arms around Finley, and squeeze. I don't care if the twins think I'm a baby. Sometimes a guy needs to hug his brother.

"How'd you find us?" he asks when I finally let him go.

"Long story. The important thing is getting you all out of here." I scan the grate above our heads with the flashlight. It's bolted in place but rusty. Maybe rusted enough to give.

"We tried that way. Couldn't get it." Trish's high-pitched voice bounces off the walls. "Is that my shoe?"

I untie the laces and hand it to her. While she wiggles her bare foot into her shoe, I bounce my flashlight from corner to corner, searching for another way out. "How'd you get in here?"

"That way." Bridgett points at the pipe where I entered.

Poised inside the pipe is a metal scorpion.

That bugger must've hidden above me as I passed him. I reach around my back, untie my shirt, and before you can say, "Take *this*, robot soldier," I've got my water gun aimed at its head.

"Mick, you shouldn't kill it." Finley's eyes keep

flicking to the side. He must want me to look where he's flicking.

"What?" I can't see it.

He faces me and points under his arm.

I stare into his armpit. Nothing there but a sweat-stained T-shirt. "What?"

I hear them before I see them.

Note to self: check debris before relaxing.

The pile of rubble unfolds, breaks apart, and scurries into position around us. Leaves uncurl into spiders. Branches untwist into centipedes. A plastic bottle shivers into a cockroach. A trick of the shadows, and a crushed shoebox creaks and stretches into Oscar.

Fear tastes like sucking on a charcoal briquette.

"The robot boy wouldn't let us tell. He said he'd kill our whole family if we told you where he was hiding. I'm sorry." Bridgett's shoulders shake and she hiccups.

"Everyone put your backs together. Make a circle. Face out." I wish I had more than one water gun. I wish I had a real weapon. All I've got is . . . my mouth. It hasn't saved us yet but I've got to keep trying. My words are all I've got left. "This is between me and you, Oscar. Call off your soldiers. Let Finley and the girls go."

Oscar glares at me with soulless mechanical eyes.

I keep talking. "Your programming. It's for me, not for them. You're not supposed to scare or harm these other kids. Only me. You have to stay true to your program."

"I make my own program." Oscar's chest rumbles.

I switch tactics and push the water gun into Finley's hands. "You bet you do. You're a smart robot. Smartest I've ever met. You captured all those people back there. What other robot could've done that? How'd you get them into the storm pipes, anyway?"

"Those people are easy to move." The rumbles die off. "Scared of our lasers and knives. Go wherever we want them to. Kids . . . more difficult. They want to fight."

"I don't want to fight anymore, Oscar. Look . . ." I hold out my empty hands. "No weapons."

"No water-propellant apparatus."

"That's right. Just me. I'm who you want. So let these other kids go." I give Finley a hip shove and hope he understands he needs to move toward the pipe while I'm keeping Oscar busy. "You don't need them, Oscar."

"Not Oscar. Oscar no longer present."

Finley slides away from me, inch by inch. He

understood! And he's got the back of Bridgett's shirt balled in his hand. She follows Finley, her hand clasped around her sister's.

"OK. Not Oscar. What do you want me to call you then?"

"General."

"General? OK, I can call you General." If I get out of this alive, I'll have to ask Savannah if she got her app off some military website.

Finley and the girls are right up against the perimeter of robot bugs. One more step and Finley will step on one.

"General, why don't you let my brother and the girls go? You don't need them. You have me. Isn't it me you want?"

"You are scared for them." The general's eyes glow brighter.

Yes! Yes! I want to scream at him. But if I say yes, Oscar—General—will know my weakness. He could hurt them just to hurt me. I could make things worse. I shuffle my feet. I stare at Finley.

My brother, he got a lot taller over the summer. And braver. I remember how he handled the other monsters we've met. How he stood up to me. How he told the truth to Savannah's dad even though he knew I'd be mad. I watch him grasp the water gun, the twins tucked in tight around him. His shoulders are stiff and strong, his chin sturdy. He nods his head like he knows what I'm thinking.

"No, General. I'm not scared for them. Not one bit. My brother can take care of himself. And he can take care of the girls. I'm not scared for the towns-people you captured, either. My friends have already rescued them. They're on their way home right now."

The general whirs and clicks, sending a cold finger down my spine. I breathe deep. At least his chest isn't rumbling up a fireball.

"Your brother and neighbors are free to leave."

The bug robots skitter out of my brother's path.

"Go. Go." He ushers Trish and Bridgett to the pipe. They crawl inside. Finley ducks and follows them.

He doesn't look back.

The robot bugs close the circle around me.

"What scares you, Mickey Bogerman?"

Good question. Robot bugs that shoot lasers. Rotten zombie corpses reaching for me in my dreams. Scaly mermaids with webbed fingers and sharp teeth. Being alone with no one to talk to, no one to back me up. Sometimes everything scares me. Sometimes nothing. I don't know if I should rattle off a list for General or go all Batman on him and punch him in the neck. He is smaller than me, after all. But there is the whole fireball issue.

"Answer, Mickey Bogerman. What scares you?"

The robot bugs push toward me. Pincers grind and spark, drill bits whir, laser nozzles glow like hundreds of demon eyes.

Over their backs, a figure crouches inside the pipe a few feet away. Did Finley come back? I hold my breath.

Savannah's hair shimmers gray in the moonlight. She uncurls her fingers. Her hand is bandaged with a torn strip from a T-shirt; the EMP box nestles in her palm.

The general's chest rumbles. The circle of orange in the center brightens like a flame. "Answer the question, Mickey Bogerman."

Savannah tosses the EMP box. It sails toward me.

Too hard. Too fast. Too far. It's gonna overshoot me and smash into the side of the basin. It's gonna crack open into a kazillion bits.

I launch myself into the air. My hands snatch the box and I crash to the floor. Thrusting the EMP at General's glowing chest, my thumb finds the raised plastic button.

"I'm not afraid of you!" I press.

I tighten all my muscles and wince, expecting a bomb explosion.

Instead, the orange circle fades to black. The light in the general's eyes winks out. He doesn't even collapse. Just stands there frozen.

The robot bugs paralyze in place like in a game of freeze tag.

I poke the general in the chest and he falls over with a clatter. "And stop calling me Mickey. My name is Mick."

Confess

BEACHWOOD GETS its fair share of tropical storms in the fall. So before the government's investigation team, the press, and a few thousand robot enthusiasts descended on our town, Hurricane Noel beat everybody back inland. The outer banks got the worst of it, but we had to board up and shut down while the winds raged. Trees got yanked out of the ground. Storm drains got flooded. And the general and his minions got washed out to sea.

Occasionally a screw or a drill bit comes in with the tide. But the robots? No one ever saw them again.

Like the storm, the stories about alien robots calmed down. Now the townspeople talk about the invasion over coffee behind closed doors instead of on every street corner. Of course, that might have something to do with the three biker guys who threaten to beat up anybody who mentions them.

Life is pretty much back to normal.

Well, for everyone but me.

I still have another day left to go on my five-day suspension from school. Yeah. It took me a couple weeks to build up the nerves to turn myself in. Let's just say Principal Nuñez was not impressed with my tactics. Even though during my confession Savannah was there with me for moral support, I got suspended anyway. She even told Principal Nuñez about Oscar.

He didn't believe her.

She's told a bunch of adults it was her fault a killer robot army invaded the town.

They pat her head and tell her what a great imagination she has.

Nope, they'd rather believe the robots were sent by aliens. Or they were part of some government conspiracy. Go figure.

I shake my head and sand down the rough spots on the wall patch in the hallway. This is the last hole I have to fix before Mom can slap on a coat of paint. Something to do during my forced vacation from school since I've read through the stack of detective books Mr. Corcoran brought over. We're still waiting on a new used refrigerator from Uncle George. In the meantime, the Garnets loaned us a mini-fridge to keep milk, but we've been eating a lot of canned stuff. Don't think my taste buds will ever recover from all the SpaghettiOs I've had to eat.

Rap, tappity, rap.

I climb down the ladder to answer the door.

Savannah reveals a big grin. "You've got smutch on your nose." She points to her own nose.

I wipe at it with the back of my hand. "How come you're not at school?"

"I had a dentist appointment this morning. Mom's waiting in the car to take me back to school now. But I wanted to give you something first. Come on." She grabs my shoes off the floor and dangles them in front of my face. "It's outside."

Now she's got my curiosity going. Maybe Oscar's body washed up on the beach or something and she brought him over for me to see. I grab my shoes and squish them on my feet.

She bounds out of my apartment, and I have to scramble to grab my keys and lock the door behind me. I meet up with her in the courtyard.

Bagel Boy launches out of the shed and slaps a big tongue swipe across my chin, sending me sprawling.

"Ugh! You saw me an hour ago. Give me a break." I ruffle the scruff of his neck.

Savannah pulls me off the ground. "Over here."

Around the side of the shed is the most awesome

sight in the whole universe.

My bike.

Showroom new.

"How?" I run my fingers across the handlebars. The blue paint on the body has metal flecks that sparkle in the sun. The black vinyl seat glows. A new chrome basket is strapped to the back.

"I found it in an alley the end of summer. When I met Finley at the beach, he told me all about your adventure with the mermaid, how you busted your bike and had to leave it behind. I figured the bike I found must be yours. I was going to fix it up for you right away. But then you were loathsome and cruel, so I left it in my garage for a while."

I don't have to look up what loathsome means.

"After Oscar went rogue and we worked together to destroy him, I started repairing it again. I finished last night and couldn't wait to give it to you."

"It's . . . it's great. But why? Why would you . . . do something so nice?"

"I thought I would help you out. Like if we were friends. 'Cause that's what friends do. Help each other. We could be friends now." She holds out her hand for a shake.

"You didn't have to fix my bike to make us friends."

How can I tell her we were friends the second she followed me out of her house to help rescue Finley? The minute she climbed the ladder to take out Oscar and she got her hand burned? The moment she threw me the EMP box? When she sat beside me in the principal's office? Honestly, I'm no hard-boiled detective who'd rather go it alone. I do better with a friend or two.

"We *are* friends, Savannah." I clasp her hand and shake. "Even though you're a girl."

Mick, Finley, and Savannah's List of Materials for Destroying the New Girl's Killer Robot Army
OR, WHAT WE LEARNED TO HAVE WITH US NEXT TIME

1. Water guns, and lots of them. Finley's idea, a good one, right?
2. A couple fire extinguishers.
3. A mirror, for deflecting laser-rays.
4. More than one folding knife, for cutting through fishnet cocoons.
5. A backpack, for shielding and for carrying anti-robot weapons.
6. A couple handfuls of dead creepy crawlies to throw on girls. Ha! Just kidding, Savannah.
7. A flashlight.
8. More than one electromagnetic pulse emitter. In case the first one gets dropped and can't be found later.
9. A wagon, for transporting supplies.
10. Sneakers, for running fast, for protecting feet, and for leaving behind as a clue.
11. A broom handle for jamming into rodent holes.
12. A dog.
13. Friends.

Come Visit Us at
www.SlugPieStories.com

Vote for the next Slug Pie Story

Send in your fan art

Share zombie killing tips and tricks

Print Mick's favorite family recipes

Download study guides for classrooms & book clubs

Learn more about your favorite characters

And more . . .

While Mick's story is fresh in your mind, would you leave us a review in your favorite review spot?

Goodreads: www.goodreads.com

Amazon: www.amazon.com

Barnes & Noble: www.BN.com

Books A Million: www.booksamillion.com

ACKNOWLEDGEMENTS

This book could not have been created without
help and inspiration from the following:

The Blaski Family and The Hockhalter Family for
their emotional and financial support.

The extraordinary Jennifer Kay and Alice Fleury
for their critiquing, and writerly love.

The Asner Family, The Morris Family, The Beasley
Family, Sharon Cooper, and The Munson Family for
their readerly love.

Michael Carr for first believing and picking this
particular writer out of the slush.

Rachel Defries, Corinne Dyuvis, and Katie Carson
for holding hands online during the
rollercoaster ride.

Amy Maddox for editing and proofreading with
scalpel precision and tender care.

Kat Powell for her exceptional talent, unending patience, and kick-rumpus illustrations.

Nic, Clarissa, and Irina for never-ending curiosity and enthusiasm.

For the writers, too numerous to mention them all, who put themselves out there every day, teaching and inspiring the rest of us.

To the readers. You are the reason.

CPSIA information can be obtained at www.ICGtesting.com
Printed in the USA
LVOW04s2139041214

417297LV00015B/412/P